DEATH TO ORDER

DEATH TO ORDER

JJ SULLIVAN

BATTERTON POLICE BOOK 2

Cover designed by Jessica Bell Design
Book design by Dean Fetzer, GunBoss Books

Printed in the United Kingdom

First Printing: March 2022
Mandrill Press

978-1-910194-32-4

PROLOGUE

DECEMBER 2002

Westwood kneels in the ditch. Behind him is Turkey; ahead is Saddam Hussein's Iraq. This, too, is Iraq, at least on the map, but for those who live here it's Kurdistan. A country recognised by Kurds and no one else.

He is waiting for Ehmed. As always at times like this, it feels as though he's been waiting for hours although the reality is he's been here for only a few minutes and Ehmed isn't yet late.

Westwood can't help it. Only activity takes his mind away from the foolishness of what he's committed to. Sitting like this, waiting for someone he's never met and doesn't know for certain he can trust is agony. Apart from which, the vicious cold of December in Iraqi Kurdistan eats at his fingers, his toes and his stomach.

And then, there's a sound behind him so soft it could be an animal going about its nocturnal business. But this animal is human.

1

Ehmed taps him on the shoulder. 'Mr Westwood. This is your last chance to go back. In twenty minutes you can be in the hotel bar in Erbil.'

Westwood shakes his head. 'Take me across.'

Chapter 1

Now

Jensen Bartholomew, well fed and self-satisfied, was Zooming with his brother, Cedric when the door behind him opened and a figure entered covered head to foot in a black gown and wearing a Guy Fawkes mask. As Jensen watched, the figure wrapped something around Cedric's neck and pulled it tight. Cedric half rose from his chair. His hands struggled to free himself and his feet stamped a furious tattoo on the worn lino beneath them, but the figure did not relent. Cedric sank out of sight. The figure leaned in close to the screen and pointed through it at Jensen. In a deep and gravelly voice, it said, 'You're next.' Then the screen went as dead as Cedric.

* * *

It took a while, because Jensen Bartholomew sat for some time staring at the screen on which he had watched his brother die. Eventually he did what he ought to do and very soon after that the Batterton Police control room put out a call to PC Jamie Pearson and his new mentee who were closest to the address Jensen had provided for Cedric. 'Attend a Grade 1 call to 24 Dryden Close. We've had a report from a Jensen Bartholomew that he has just seen on Zoom his brother, Cedric Bartholomew, strangled at that address. We are trying to get more information but please attend with caution. We are trying to arrange back up.'

Control next checked which car was closest to Jensen Bartholomew's home and gave that car the same information adding, 'Jensen Bartholomew lives at 15, Oxford Place.' The caller would have liked to say, "Be a good pair of lads and make sure he really is where he says he is," but messages between Control and police cars follow a certain formula, and so the actual message said, 'Speak to the informant and obtain more information.'

It took Jamie and his partner four minutes to reach 24, Dryden Close, and another four to accept that no one was going to answer their knock and force entry. Three minutes later, the control room informed Detective Inspector Susanna David of a suspicious death. 'SOCO are on their way. PC Jamie Pearson is securing the scene.'

It was unusual to name the constable stringing blue and white tape around the scene, and Susanna knew why it had been done this time. Control were offering her the opportunity to take with her Jamie Pearson's wife, the fairly new DC Theresa Pearson. After a moment's thought, she called for DS Rayyan Padgett and DC Nicola Hayward. The decision had nothing to do with Theresa's competence. Padgett and Hayward were a proven team who had worked together successfully in the past and would again in the future. Theresa's time would come.

In any case, the crime scene was not where they were going first. She said, 'You know what it's like. The crime scene manager can't even get the rest of the SOCOs in there until the photographer has photographed every damn thing. Then they do their mapping and we can't set foot through the door until they've worked out a path and put down markers for us to step on. There's no rush – just as long as we get there before anyone moves the body. And Charlie is CSM, and he knows better than to let that happen before I arrive. There's somewhere else you two can go first. The brother says he has the whole thing on video. Check that out. He'll be pleased to see you – the uniforms who went there said he didn't want to let them go. While you're out, I'll have someone set up an incident room and I'll ask Superintendent McAvoy to assign a Senior Investigating Officer. And I'll try to get Marion Trimble as our HOLMES receiver. They don't come more reliable than Marion.'

As they hurried down the stairs towards the car park, Nicola said, 'The DI always refers to the Super as some kind of abstraction. Do you think she imagines we don't know they're an item?'

'She isn't that daft,' said Rayyan. 'She's just being professional. Making sure their relationship doesn't affect work.'

'They must have very interesting pillow talk.'

* * *

When they identified themselves to Jensen Bartholomew, his relief was visible. 'I've been on tenterhooks, waiting for him to turn up here.'

'Him, sir?' asked Rayyan.

'The killer. He said I'd be next.'

'Yes, sir. I see. May we come in?' The room into which he showed them was a little under-furnished for Rayyan's taste, which veered towards his Malaysian mother's liking for swagged curtains and rich fabrics. The best description for this room was "spartan," though it was expensive spartan – Jensen Bartholomew was clearly not short of a few bob, or a willingness to spend it. Rayyan said, 'Do you know who the man is?'

'I've no idea at all. He was covered from head to foot and he was wearing a mask. But I'll show you.' He led them

6

to a laptop on a table. 'It's still switched on. I'll fast forward to where this maniac comes in.'

Rayyan said, 'I have to ask you not to touch it, sir. It's evidence of a crime and I'm afraid we need to seize the laptop.'

'I can't show it to you now?'

'You shouldn't touch it again, sir. And we won't watch it ourselves. It will be turned over to our digital forensics team.'

'But...'

'I'm sorry, sir. But what is on your laptop amounts to evidence of a very serious crime, and we have to make sure that, if it is ever shown to a jury, no defence counsel can challenge the chain of evidence.' To make his meaning clearer, he moved between Bartholomew and the laptop and said to Nicola, 'We need an evidence bag large enough to hold this.'

Bartholomew looked a little bereft. He held up a flash drive. 'I've copied all the files onto here for you to take away with you. I thought that would be enough.'

Rayyan said, 'Thank you, sir, but if what is on here becomes evidence, the court isn't going to accept a copy. Any defence counsel worth their salt would get your brother's killer off. I don't suppose the CPS would even be prepared to bring a charge.'

Bartholomew shrugged. 'Well, if you must, you must. And I suppose it's a good job I recorded the call.'

'Aren't Zoom calls always recorded?'

'Not by default, but mine are. If you only want the occasional chat with a friend and it isn't going to last too long, you don't have to pay anything. But I use this for business and we sometimes have long and involved meetings with a number of people, so I have the paid-for version. And I record all of them as a matter of course. That's useful for business meetings, because it means I don't need a secretary taking notes and producing minutes. And it's even more useful where my brother's concerned. Cedric is not the most reliable person on the planet and there have been times when I've been glad to be able to prove he said something.' He looked suddenly chastened. 'I mean, wasn't. He wasn't the most reliable person. He isn't any kind of person now. Is he?'

Rayyan decided that that was best ignored. He sometimes thought that, for pathologist Professor Baines, you only really became a person after you were dead when he could cut you up and learn things about you your most intimate partner didn't know. He said, 'Mr Bartholomew. You live here, and your brother lives in Dryden Close. That's… What? Two miles away? Do you mind me asking why you zoomed?'

'Instead of meeting, you mean? Simple. I wouldn't drive there for fear of the wheels being removed from my car while I was inside. And I banned Cedric from ever setting foot in this house again. You look surprised. My brother was light fingered. He'd steal, just for the sake of stealing. I became fed up with it. Fortunately, I knew which pawnbroker he used. It wasn't difficult – there's one not a hundred yards from his house. Cedric would come here, he'd leave, I'd notice something was missing, I'd go and see the pawnbroker and buy it back. For Cedric, it was just a way of boosting his income. For me, it was a damned nuisance.'

Rayyan said, 'You mentioned business. What sort of business are you in, sir?'

Bartholomew opened a drawer and took out a handful of brochures. 'This kind.'

Rayyan glanced at them. Words like "logistics" and "global partnership" looked back at him. He said, 'Thank you. We'll take these with us. Mr Bartholomew, can you suggest any reason why someone would want to kill your brother?'

'Yes. I can. My brother was a pain in the arse and he caused a lot of trouble to a lot of people. What I can't suggest is why anyone who wanted to kill him would also want to kill me.'

9

'Was he involved in your business?'

Bartholomew sighed. 'Telling you about Cedric might take a while. And I'm sorry, I haven't offered you coffee. Let's go into the kitchen.'

Having seen the minimalist but costly room they had just been in, the kitchen came as no surprise. Large, spacious, full of every modern device and with lots of room to hold them. But the first thing a visitor noticed was the height of the ceiling – the kitchen occupied two floors. When he saw Rayyan and Nicola staring, Bartholomew said, 'Tuna. I love tuna.'

'Sir?' said Rayyan.

'Almost any restaurant that serves tuna, it's grey and cooked right through. That's no way to eat it. The perfect tuna steak is burned almost black on the outside and meltingly raw in the centre. See, what you have to do, you have to get the temperature on top of the stove up so high it begins to glow red. You need a professional stove for that. And, as you see, I have one. You spread a little oil on one side of the tuna steak, put it right on the heat, count slowly to five, turn it over and count to five again. Slap it on a warm plate and eat it right away – ideally with a fresh salad and maybe some new potatoes. Restaurants can't cook it like that because they'd set off the fire alarm. So, when I was having this house built, I had the kitchen designed over two stories.'

'Because of tuna,' said Nicola.

'Because of tuna. Of course, the alternative would be to cook it outside on a barbecue. But this is Britain and our summers are British summers. And as for our winters…'

Rayyan said, 'Do you live here alone, sir?'

'A lot of the time. I think what you're asking is: Is there a Mrs Bartholomew? Am I married? And the answer is, no, I'm not. I do, occasionally, meet someone I want to spend time with and, if she's willing, she moves in here with me for a while. But I'm afraid I bore easily. Please sit down.'

He tipped some coffee beans into a grinder on top of a machine that would not have looked out of place in an Italian coffee bar and busied himself warming milk with jets of steam. Rayyan would have loved to feel that money and effort had been expended for very little purpose. But he couldn't. He couldn't remember when he'd last had coffee as good as this. He said, holding up the brochures, 'This business, sir. Is it yours?'

'Lock stock and barrel. Cedric and I were born to a father who made a lot of money exporting things to other countries and importing other things to this country. Both Cedric and I worked in the business. Our father was a widower when he died, and he left everything equally between me and Cedric. I set up a new company and went on working as hard as I had for my father. Every penny I earned went back into the business until I had all the contacts, all the equipment, all the stock and all the storage space I needed and I didn't owe anyone anything. Cedric set out to have the best time he possibly could. I built a reasonable competence into a great deal of money. Cedric spent everything he had and then persuaded me to give him a job. It didn't work out. The only bit of the job Cedric was interested in was the salary. He didn't see why he should get off his backside or even out of bed just because I was paying him. A couple of times, he asked me to pay off debts, the size of which astounded me. The third time, I said I wouldn't. I was about to sack him; fortunately, he resigned in a rage. Told me everything I had I had by luck and if I had the slightest humanity I'd share with him fifty fifty.'

Nicola said, 'Was he married, sir?'

'Divorced. Her name is Melody Fitzgerald and the last I knew she'd bought an apartment downtown. I couldn't tell you the address but I'm sure you can find it.'

Nicola copied the name into her tablet. 'She doesn't use the Bartholomew name?'

'Why would she? They aren't married any longer.'

'How did you get on with her?'

'It wasn't my job to get on with her or not get on with her – she married my brother, not me. But how he failed to see her for the tart she was is beyond me.'

Rayyan said, 'Sir. You said you could think of a number of people who might have wanted to kill your brother. Could you tell me who they are, please?'

There was the sound of a subdued telephone ringing and Bartholomew said, 'I'll do my best. But let me take this, first. I've been waiting for this call.' Into the phone, he said, 'Daisy. Thanks for calling back. Look, I'm not going into detail right now because I have the police here, but someone has threatened my life. Yes, Daisy, my life – and I'm taking it seriously, because whoever it was has already killed Cedric. Yes. Yes, I understand your shock and I feel much the same, but right now I need you to do something. When we had that delegation from Mozambique, we used a private security company to look after them. Remember? Right. I can't recall the name of the company, but I'm sure you can find it. Tell them I need 24-hour cover. Okay? Don't call me back, Jenny – when it's fixed up, send me an email and tell me everything I need to know.' He put down the phone. 'There. That's taken care of. I can't ask for 24-hour police protection, can I? Now. You want to know who might have wanted to do away with Cedric. I hope you've got plenty of space on that thing.'

Rayyan said, 'Well, just a moment, sir. Your protection *is* our business. We'll need to send our specialists to look this place over, and they will advise on necessary security measures. I imagine we'll want to monitor your house at the very least. And, of course, we'll be appointing a family liaison officer. That's just standard procedure.'

'A family liaison officer? You mean you expect me to have a police officer living in this house with me?'

'They wouldn't live with you, sir. Most families who have suffered a blow like this have never experienced anything like it before and will probably never experience anything like it again. The FLO spends time with you to help you understand what's happening, and why.' He saw no need to add that the officer would also act as the police's eyes and ears in the house. Would that be a problem, sir?'

'Not when you describe it like that. But you make your recommendations and I'll tell you what I'm prepared to accept. And I'll still employ a security company paid by me. I don't think anything is going to substitute for that.'

CHAPTER 2

When Rayyan and Nicola got back to the station, Susanna said, 'Nicola, you stay here and give all the details you collected to Marion so she can get them onto HOLMES. DCI Blazeley has been appointed SIO and he wants to hold a briefing in two hours. The press release is out, so no doubt we'll be hearing from Bernadette Spence from the *Post* sometime soon, and the coroner has been informed. The rest of the murder team is being assembled. Rayyan, you and I have just got time to get over to the crime scene and back. On the way there, you can tell me what Jensen Bartholomew had to say.'

But he had hardly got started when they reached Dryden Close and Susanna said, 'Save the rest, Rayyan. You'll only have to go through it all again at the briefing, anyway. Or Nicola will. And people can read it on HOLMES – if I know Nicola, she won't have missed a thing when she was briefing Marion.'

Rayyan looked around. 'This is a hell of a lot different from Oxford Place.'

'Where the brother lives? Tell me?'

'Well… Look at it. You can't get much lower than this street without being in a Salvation Army hostel. And the brother's place – I don't know what he paid for it but he can't have got much change out of a couple of million.'

It was true; weeds were growing through cracks in the pavement, some windows had been boarded up and none of the front doors looked as though they had seen fresh paint for a long time. Identifying the house where Cedric had died was easy enough because PC Jamie Pearson occupied the doorway. A bunch of kids, and one or two adults of both sexes, were staring, as if waiting for an entertainment to start. Jamie logged the two visitors, both of whom he recognised without asking for their warrant cards.

'Jamie,' said Susanna with a nod. 'Any trouble?'

'Nothing. I don't think they have the energy.'

'Has anyone started door-to-door?'

The ghost of a smile touched Jamie's lips. 'DCI Blazeley sent four officers. Two of them are halfway down that way,' he said, pointing in one direction, and then he pointed in the other. 'And two that way. I don't think they are getting much help. Which is amazing, when you think about it – a man in a cloak and a mask arrives in a street like this, goes through a door like that and throttles someone to death, and no one sees a thing.'

Susanna said, 'I wonder if he walked down the street or came by car?'

Jamie shook his head. 'Whichever it was, I don't think anyone's telling.'

Susanna peered through the door. SOCO's stepping plates were on the floor. She said, 'Where's the body?'

'Ground floor, back room,' said Jamie.

When she and Rayyan reached there, Charlie, the crime scene manager, was supervising his team. 'What a dump,' he said when he saw them. 'This is the kind of place where you wipe your shoes when you're leaving. He's here.' He stepped back so they could see Cedric Bartholomew's body on the floor. 'The ligature is still round his neck.'

'What is it?' asked Susanna.

'It's a very thin, very flexible, very strong wire. Piano wire? Could be. We'll know more in due course. There's a loop at one end and the rest of the wire is pulled through that. Once it was round his neck and pulled tight, he won't have had a chance. Especially as he doesn't look particularly fit. But the pathologist will be able to tell you more about that.'

'Indeed. Anything else I should know?'

'I heard you'll be able to watch the whole thing on video. Or was that an exaggeration?'

'Not at all. So we'll know how it was done and, for once in our lives, time of death won't be an issue – we'll know exactly when he died. The only two things we won't know are who killed him, and why.'

'I'm afraid I can't help you there. Am I okay to get the body removed to the mortuary?'

'Go ahead. I'll just have a poke around and then go.'

The bedroom contained a bed, a chair, a table, two pairs of jeans, much worn, three pairs of Y fronts of which two needed to be washed, and five T-shirts that looked as though they had been around a long time. Three had advertising slogans on the front. When they reached the kitchen, Susanna said, 'The homes of the poor tell you so much more than the homes of the rich.'

Rayyan, who knew exactly what she meant but also knew the value of humouring the boss, said, 'In what way?'

'Remember Terence Carpenter? Well, how could you forget him? Carpenter had more money than anyone could possibly need, he employed a gardener, he paid a cleaning agency – if you remember, he gave the cleaner a seeing to and he paid money to her brother to avoid any trouble afterwards. There was nothing in the house to give us a lead. Whereas here...' Rayyan was thinking that there was only nothing in Carpenter's house to give Major Crimes a lead if you discounted a safe containing photographs of illegal sex acts with a minor, but Susanna was in full flow. '... Here, we've got a sink with no dirty dishes in it, no pans...'

'There weren't any of those at Carpenter's place, either.'

'No, but the difference is that Carpenter didn't have a fridge so old it had stopped working and doesn't even have a bottle of milk in it. Carpenter didn't have cupboards without a single thing you could eat in any of them.' She opened the back door and asked the SOCO working there, 'Has this bin been done yet?' When he nodded, she lifted the lid and said, 'Carpenter didn't have the wrappers from petrol station sandwiches with stamps on saying the price has been marked down because they were out of time.' She stepped back into the kitchen. 'Carpenter had expensive wine and whisky in his house and Cedric Bartholomew doesn't even have the cheap kind of alcohol – have you seen an empty lager can? Me neither.' She sniffed. 'And Carpenter's house didn't have the faint aroma of marijuana hanging about the place, or the makings for roll-ups. I wonder what other drugs he might have consumed. No doubt it will be ages before we get the toxicology report back to tell us. Which reminds me: You can have the pleasure of the post-mortem in my place. And take Theresa Pearson with you. I don't think she's done a PM yet. Let's get back to the station.'

* * *

Susanna had said that the homes of the poor told the observer more than the homes of the rich. True for the police, that was also true for journalists. When Bernadette Spence, crime reporter at the *Post*, went to interview the well-to-do Jensen Bartholomew (as she would), he would simply tell her to talk to his company's press officer. The rich were protected from the press and told them only what they wanted them to know. It was different for the poor. And not only because the poor had no intermediaries to place between them and an inquisitive reporter. Cedric Bartholomew's neighbours had told the officers making door-to-door enquiries nothing. That had not been the result of prior agreement – it was Dryden Close's standard operating procedure. Telling coppers nothing was always the safe option. You couldn't get into trouble if you kept your trap shut. Children learned that before they learned to tie their shoelaces.

Talking to journalists was different. Journalists spoke to the world, not to the courts. They did it through newspapers, the radio and television. Talking to a journalist didn't get you into trouble and it might get you on TV for your fifteen minutes of fame.

And so it was that the first story the *Post* carried about the murder of Cedric Bartholomew contained rather more information than the police had been able to gather.

Brother Watches Brother's Brutal Murder

Bernadette Spence

Police were called today to Dryden Close after Batterton businessman and millionaire Jensen Bartholomew watched his brother, Cedric Bartholomew, strangled to death while the two were talking to each other on Zoom. Cedric's neighbours said they thought nothing of it when a man dressed head to foot in a flowing black robe and wearing a Guy Fawkes mask arrived on a vintage Triumph motorbike and let himself into Cedric's home using a key. It was only when police arrived and began asking questions that they discovered that their neighbour had been brutally murdered.

Patrick Brennan, who lives next door, described Cedric as a quiet person who kept himself to himself. 'I moved in here three years ago and Cedric was already living next door. I don't believe we've exchanged more than twenty words in all that time.' Another neighbour, who did not wish to be named, said that Cedric was generally known to be the brother of a very wealthy man and was said to have been rich himself at one time. 'He didn't really belong around here. He'd obviously had a good education, but he had come down in the world. I assumed there were mental health issues, but I don't know that for sure. He didn't look after himself, and no one else was doing it for him.'

Enquiries to social services reveal that Cedric Bartholomew was not known to them, for mental health or any other reasons. Jensen Bartholomew, the dead man's brother, lives in upper-class Oxford Place in a house estimated to be worth more than two million pounds. A spokesman for Mr Bartholomew said there was no reason to suppose whoever killed his brother might also seek to attack Mr Bartholomew. The spokesman said that he worked for the Albion Agency and that he had begun work shadowing Mr Bartholomew only today. The Albion Agency provides bodyguards and physical security.

That information, though a lot more than the police had been given, had some shortcomings. The vintage Triumph, for example, had actually been neither vintage nor a Triumph, but there was a limit to how truthful it was possible to be. The police would read Bernie Spence's story and nobody in Dryden Close wanted to give her anything that might really help them. And then there was the description of Cedric as a quiet person who kept himself to himself. That was somewhat at odds with the general recollection. And Patrick Brennan, who had given it, was being a little economical with the truth when he said they'd only exchanged twenty words in three years; Cedric had asked Patrick to "keep the fucking noise down, you smear of faecal Irish slime," at least once a week for the whole of those three years thanks to Patrick's habit of spending most of his dole money on the cheapest wine money could buy and then carousing in his back garden with BBC Radio One at full blast until he passed out.

* * *

Jenny Frobisher was MP for the constituency of which Batterton was at the centre. When her agent wanted to speak to her, as he did now with some urgency, he found it relatively easy because he was her husband and even easier when – as now – Parliament was in recess and Jenny was spending seven days out of each week at home. He placed a copy of *The Post* in front of her. Jenny looked at the headline and said, 'Cedric Bartholomew? Did we know him? Is he related to the odious Jensen Bartholomew?'

'Yes to the second question. He is his brother. To the first – did we know him? Not directly. But he did a job for us.'

'Which was?'

'Those files. The ones you felt we should recover from the lawyers you found every bit as odious as you find Jensen Bartholomew. Cedric Bartholomew was there with the man I hired. A man whose particular gift was getting into places whose owner would prefer that people didn't.'

Jenny considered this information in silence. Then she said, 'I have to go out. I have a surgery. What joy – all those ill-informed and prejudiced constituents to talk to. When I get back, Harold, dear, I'd like a briefing on just who might know of this tenuous connection between us and a dead man. And briefings should be short, Harold. The clue is in the name.'

CHAPTER 3

Detective Chief Inspector George Blazeley was senior investigating officer on the case and, when he opened the briefing, he had the *Post*'s story in front of him. 'Who did the door-to-door?'

Four uniformed officers held up their hands.

'Then can you tell me how a woman on her own with no official authority at all was able to find out that the killer arrived on a motorbike when you couldn't?'

'No, sir.'

'Marion, an action on HOLMES, please. Find the name of the owner of every Triumph motorbike built before 1980 and registered within fifty miles of the centre of Batterton. Then give these four the task of locating each one of those bikes and collecting the owner's alibi for this morning.'

A DS said, 'Sir, do we have a view on Jensen Bartholomew retaining the services of a bodyguard?'

'Yes, Brendan, we do. Jensen Bartholomew is as entitled as any other British citizen to employ someone to provide him with physical protection. The only proviso is that the bodyguard must not be armed and that any force used in Mr Bartholomew's interest must be proportionate. Now, what else do we have? The video of the Zoom conversation and the killing that ended it. The video has been transcribed, but we will watch the whole of it from the beginning, including what the brothers were saying to each other, and then we will discuss what we think we saw and heard. So pay close attention.'

The lights in the room were turned low and the film began to play on a large screen that everyone in the incident room could see. While they were watching, Theresa handed round the printed transcript of the conversation between the two brothers. At the end, Blazeley said, 'Any comments?'

A DS raised his hand. 'Three times, Cedric says he can't go on like this, but he never says what "like this" means.'

'That's right,' said Blazeley. 'He doesn't. Anyone got any ideas?'

Nicola said, 'He means he needs money.'

'Yes,' said the DS. 'And he thinks his brother should provide it. But what does he need it for? He doesn't say. According to what Rayyan and the DI have put on HOLMES, he was eating almost nothing. Out-of-date sandwiches. Nothing in the fridge, and the fridge wouldn't have kept it cool anyway. No alcohol, which is probably unique in that street. The cheapest possible smokes, and I bet he didn't indulge in very many.'

'There were no filled ashtrays,' said Susanna.

'Exactly. What was he living on? Did he have a job? Was he on benefits? How much did he take home each week, and what was he spending it on?'

Blazeley said, 'Those are good questions, Mahmoud. Marion, put them on HOLMES and task Mahmoud and a DC of his choice to get the answers.'

'Taffy and I work well together,' said Mahmoud.

'Taffy it shall be,' said Blazeley. 'You'll need authorisation from a superintendent to collect bank and credit card details and his benefit records – I'll see you get it. Charlie. there's been no mention of a laptop. What did he Zoom on?'

'There was no computer of any kind,' said the CSM. 'He used a Samsung smartphone. We've confirmed that it belonged to Jensen Bartholomew's company, and they paid the bills. I've got a telecoms unit looking at it right now to find out who the victim called, who called him, and what he stored on it. I've asked for a rush job; I should have the answers for you by morning.'

'Good man,' said Blazeley.

'But this laptop you brought in from Jensen Bartholomew's house. The one we've just been watching the Zoom call on.'

'What about it?'

'According to Rayyan,' said Charlie, 'Jensen Bartholomew bought this for the sole purpose of speaking to his brother on it. Why?'

Rayyan said, 'I assumed it had special features of some kind.'

'That's just the point,' said Charlie. 'It has no special features of any description. One of the richest men in the county bought this laptop and it's just about the cheapest device on the market.'

Blazeley said, 'I suppose that tells us what he thought of his brother. He wasn't worth more.'

'Maybe,' said Charlie. 'I can tell you, that is all he used it for. I looked at the hard drive and there's nothing else on there. It has a standard copy of Windows, but he hasn't even set it up for emails.'

'Interesting,' said Blazeley. 'And a pity, because we might find it useful to take a closer look at Jensen Bartholomew's business. If we had grounds we could seize any other laptops and computers he has. But we don't, so we'll have to go with what we have. Rayyan and Theresa probably won't be back from the post-mortem for another couple of hours. Susanna and I will wait to hear what they have to say. The rest of you, get your assigned actions from Marion and get on with them. When you're done, go home – you'll need a break. Everyone here tomorrow morning at six thirty, please, for the morning briefing. Bacon sandwiches will be provided. For those who can't eat bacon, the sandwiches will be egg. If you can't eat egg or bacon, bring your own. But don't be late.'

After the meeting had broken up, Susanna asked Blazeley, 'Do you think Bartholomew knows more than he's letting on?'

'Too early to say. When we find out why Cedric Bartholomew was killed, we'll know whether Jensen Bartholomew should have been able to point us in the right direction. Until then... Who knows? Right now, I should be going upstairs to bring the Super up to speed. Do you want to do it?'

Susanna knew Blazeley would not have asked anyone else that question. She had often wondered how much people knew about her relationship with Superintendent Chris McAvoy, but Chris had told her that whatever level of knowledge she thought there was would be an underestimate. 'This is a police force, darling. It's made up of people who get paid for observing other people and drawing conclusions from their behaviour. They don't stop doing it when they walk through the police station door. I don't suppose there's a single person in the building who doesn't know you and I are an item. Does it bother you?'

She was floored for a moment. 'I don't know. Should it?'

'It doesn't bother me.'

Then she wouldn't let it bother her. And let's face it, she needed a word with Chris because they weren't going to do much talking this evening. The first few days of a murder enquiry, the DI got home to sleep, shower and put on clean clothes. Not much else. Whereas, once you reached Chris's elevated level, you followed most people's idea of normal office hours. 'Yes,' she said. 'I would like to be the one to update the Super.'

No trace of anything passed across Blazeley's face. All he said was, 'Go and do it. When you get back, Rayyan and Theresa may have the initial post-mortem results for us.'

* * *

Ali Badaan could have been feeling better. It wasn't the beer he'd drunk – Ali had squared his conscience about drinking alcohol years ago. It wasn't even the slice of crisp bacon on the burger he'd eaten in the pub for lunch – he told himself that Mohammed, peace be upon him, had forbidden eating anything off a pig because when he lived fifteen hundred years ago there had been no refrigeration, pig meat went off very quickly in hot weather, and not many places got as hot as Arabia. If you lived in this benighted, godless but above all cold country, the ban need not apply to you. Especially if you had refrigerators, which the pub certainly did. No, what was troubling Ali was the knowledge that he'd seen Westwood when he came to kill Cedric Bartholomew, and he'd recognised him. Or, if he hadn't, he'd recognised the bike. And he thought Westwood probably knew that. Whether Westwood would want to do anything about it, he didn't know. And he wasn't in a hurry to find out.

His phone ringing brought relief, partly because it took his mind away from what had been worrying him but mostly because the caller was offering him a job. He listened to what she had to say. You needed a good memory for this work, because you could never write the details down and turning up at the wrong address could be disastrous. 'Yes,' he said. 'Tonight, an hour after it gets dark. How much?'

'Two fifty,' said the caller. 'When you've done the job, stay there until the customer shows up. He'll have the money with him.'

Ali said, 'I usually get paid in advance, so I don't have to meet…' He tailed off when he realised the caller had hung up.

He'd have preferred cash in his hand, but he understood the customer's reservations. This had not been one of his regular callers. In fact, he'd never spoken to her before. Most jobs came from Terry Winkleman, and Winkleman knew his work. Knew how reliable he was. You couldn't blame someone you hadn't worked for before for not wanting to part with the money until they could see the job had been done. For all they knew, Ali might be a drunk who'd spend the money and forget to turn up. In any case, he was feeling better. That was how it was in Ali's world – you couldn't worry too long about something that only might happen, and not many worries could survive the promise of two hundred and fifty pounds in a few hours time. He'd spend some of it on an hour with a woman. Not the sort of woman who showed up in the pub at the end of Dryden Close – a woman with soft pink skin who washed her clothes and whispered encouragement while he was on top of her. He knew those endearments weren't meant, they were just part of the deal, but they made him feel good for all that. He hadn't felt that kind of good for a little too long.

And speaking of clean clothes... He checked his back pocket. Fifty quid. He went back into the pub and walked through to the room at the back. The Mahoney kid was still there. Ali made sure he caught his eye and then wagged his head in the direction of the exit into the back yard. There was no response, but he knew the Mahoney kid had got the message. Ali walked out into the yard. Two minutes or so later, the kid followed him. Ali said, 'That blue-and-white striped jacket you talked about. You've got it in my size?'

The look the kid gave him might have been from a professional tailor. 'Medium, regular arm length? Sure, I've got your size.'

'And it's new. And looks like it's new.'

'Never been worn. Straight out of the store. You'll look like a king's ransom.'

Ali handed over twenty pounds. 'I need it this evening.'

'It'll be hanging from your back door handle ten minutes from now.'

Ali nodded. 'Good man.'

'She'll think you're a gangster. She'll be eating out of your hand.'

Ali said, 'It's not my hand I want her to eat.' But the kid was already gone.

* * *

At that time of year, an hour after it got dark meant nine thirty in the evening. DI Susanna David was still twenty minutes from being able to go home, but she now knew a lot more about Cedric Bartholomew's physical condition at the time of his death than she had before. She didn't know much more than that. But now it was time to wrap up for the night.

Ali Badaan, on the other hand, was starting work. He'd arrived at the office building on the edge of town from which Jensen Bartholomew's business operated. His arrival had been preceded by that of Del Theobald. Ali had little time for people like Del, who he regarded as an uneducated and brainless thug, though (or because of which) face-to-face he always treated Del with respect. Del would never have fitted into a medium jacket, regular arm length, because he was built like a gorilla, though he was in every other way as unlike that peaceable primate as it's possible to imagine. His job had been to incapacitate the night watchman, which he had done by the simple process of hitting him on the head with a thick woollen sock filled with heavy weights. In fact, though Del didn't know it, he'd hit him so hard that the watchman was never going to recover consciousness. He'd dragged his victim into the row of trees that provided a tasteful barrier between the building and the road and sat down to wait. Del's fee for his part of the job was a hundred pounds and, unlike Ali, he had been paid in advance, but Del liked to know everything that went on. You never knew when you might need knowledge you were not supposed to have.

Ali prided himself that his work required less brawn than Del's, but more brain. It was to render ineffective the expensive and sophisticated alarm systems that were supposed to prevent unauthorised entry to the building. This was something Ali was very good at. He'd often thought, in his more reflective moments (which usually meant when he'd smoked something he shouldn't have been smoking after drinking to excess) that, if he'd continued in the path his parents had mapped out for him, he could now be a very large cheese in a big company and living in one of those expensive houses in Oxford Place. But he'd found after leaving university with his degree in electronic engineering that you didn't get to the very large cheese stage until you'd been through a number of years – quite a large number – of routine work doing what other people told you to do. Ali had never much liked doing what other people told him to do. So now he lived in Dryden Close where, until the last twenty-four hours, his neighbours had included Cedric Bartholomew.

It was only when he read the *Post* that day, having contributed to it the deliberately inaccurate information about the make and age of the motorbike, that he realised that the Bartholomew brothers shared that mixture of places: one of them lived in Oxford Place and the other in Dryden Close. Ali didn't make anything of that; the romance and poetry of life had never interested him.

Now he went about his work, confident in his ability and in his dress – the blue and white jacket had been an excellent fit and he had no doubt that some lucky girl in a club tonight would be delighted to go with him. A lucky professional girl – Ali's record with girls who didn't charge had never been good.

It took only six minutes before every alarm was bypassed. Quietly but professionally pleased with his performance, Ali opened the front door and left it open. That was the signal to the client who was no doubt watching from somewhere from which he could make a quick getaway if Ali had botched his part of the job. He sat down in a corner of reception to await the arrival of his two hundred and fifty pounds.

A shadow flitted across the car park in front of the building. It pressed against the wall, slid sideways towards the door, and entered. And Ali's entrails turned to water. Something not entirely dissimilar had happened to Del Theobald. There weren't many faces that could strike terror into Del, but this was one of them. He left in a greater hurry than he usually showed about anything.

'Ali! Nice threads!'

'Westwood?' It came out so quietly, he had to say it again. 'Westwood? My God, man, where have you been? I haven't seen you for – oh, so long, I can't remember.'

'Now, Ali, that isn't quite true, is it? Have you checked upstairs?'

What did he mean by, "that isn't quite true"? But Ali wasn't really in any doubt. 'Upstairs? Of course. You know me, Westwood – you pay your money and you get what you pay for. In spades. And no comeback afterwards. Never, Westwood – no one has ever had to worry about Ali Badaan after they've done a job. I'm the number one no-grass operator. I've never grassed anyone up in my life.'

Westwood placed a hand on Ali's shoulder, and Ali thought he would sink into the floor. The hand was encased in the kind of blue nitrile glove hospital workers wear. Westwood said, 'I know that. I know you wouldn't grass. I thought it was very clever, the way you lied to the reporter about the bike. That was you, wasn't it?'

Unable to trust himself to speak, Ali nodded.

'Let's go upstairs, Ali. There's something I want us to look at together.'

All Ali wanted was to get out of there alive. He knew Westwood didn't believe he would ever grass him up. But he also knew Westwood didn't like loose ends. That was why he'd been so worried earlier today. And Westwood was probably the only psychopath Ali was aware of ever having met. If Westwood thought killing Ali was a better bet than letting him live, Ali was a dead man. 'Listen, Westwood, someone's waiting for me. A girl. I've done my job; whatever you want to do in here, you're free to do it. Just let me have the cash and I'll be off.' He knew his voice was wavering; he was begging to be spared.

'A girl! Now I understand the smart threads. You don't pull on a jacket like that just to open up an office building for me. Well, you rascal!' He took an envelope from his pocket and placed it in Ali's hands. 'There's your pay, Ali. Enjoy your evening.' And then his right hand was pointing away from him, and there was a click, and a blade more than six inches long protruded suddenly from his hand and Ali's throat was cut from one side all the way to the other.

The first person would not arrive to find the bodies of Ali and the nightwatchman until eight in the morning, by which time the briefing on the Cedric Bartholomew case was already over.

Rayyan had reported back on the post-mortem, but all that told them was that Cedric had died as a result of strangulation, that he'd been undernourished for a long period, that his teeth did not appear to have been looked after for some time and were likely to have been giving him trouble, and that he suffered from haemorrhoids.

'Lovely,' murmured one of the older DCs.

'We should have toxicology reports in a couple of days,' said Rayyan. 'Other than that... There's nothing to say. There was nothing to suggest any kind of serious illness.'

'Thank you, Rayyan,' said Blazeley. 'Mahmoud, the Super has authorised you and Taffy to do whatever you need to to find out how much money the victim had coming in, and what he did with it. Charlie, do you have anything for us?'

'It's early days,' said the crime scene manager. 'The phone was three months old. I've given Marion a list of the numbers that were called from it during that time, and the numbers that called it. There isn't a single photograph. No cats, no selfies, no genitalia – his own or anyone else's. And none have been deleted. It's a very nice phone with all sorts of clever features like notepads, calculators and diaries, and none of them have been used.'

'Marion, we need someone checking out who called him and who he called ASAP. Anything else, Charlie?'

'As you might imagine, there were fingerprints all over the place. It will take a while to sort through them all; Professor Baines took the victim's fingerprints as part of the post-mortem, so we have those for elimination purposes.'

Blazeley said, 'I wonder if Jensen Bartholomew ever went there? Susanna, you'll be sending someone to talk to him again – get them to ask for his fingerprints. Might be necessary to use a little tact. Who's checking out the victim's ex-wife?'

Rayyan said, 'Nicola and me. Her name is Melody Fitzgerald. She was out when we went round there yesterday evening at eight, and she was still out two hours later. We left a note asking her to make contact, but we'll call back there as soon as this meeting is over.'

'What sort of place does she live in?' asked Susanna.

'One of those nifty apartments that went up five years ago overlooking the river. Where the grain store used to be.'

'Not cheap,' said Susanna. 'She can't be suffering financially the way her ex was.'

'No,' said Nicola. 'And she has a penthouse.' Everyone in the force knew that Nicola lived in a maisonette and was only able to keep up the mortgage payments by taking in a lodger. Her obvious feelings about the difference between her own accommodation and Melody Fitzgerald's raised smiles around the room.

'You'll get there, Nicola,' said Blazeley. 'Okay, I think that's it for now. We'll meet again at six this afternoon.'

But they hadn't yet the phone call about the body of Ali Badaan.

CHAPTER 4

Susanna, flanked on one side by Rayyan and on the other by Nicola, stared at the bloody spectacle before them. Ali Badaan was sitting in a chair in reception for anyone who came through the door to see him. The collar and lapels of the pristine blue and white striped jacket were soaked in red. His hands had been folded in his lap around an envelope. Two uniformed officers had erected crime scene tape covering the whole area from the trees lining the road to the boundary wall behind the building and were recording all visitors to the site. SOCO were hard at work, starting in the reception area and at the tree line. Reception now being a crime scene, Jensen Bartholomew and a man Susanna took to be his bodyguard were in chairs that had been brought out into the car park. A woman apparently in a state of extreme nervous exhaustion sat beside them.

Susanna said, 'Who found them?'

Sally Christmas, crime scene manager at this scene, pointed at Ali. 'He was found first. By the lady over there – the one in tears. Fortunately for you, the screaming stopped before you got here. She's the receptionist and she walked straight through the door to see that. When Mr Bartholomew got here, he wanted to know why there was no sign of a nightwatchman, so the lads in uniform had a look and they found him in the trees.'

'This guy's name was Ali Badaan.'

'You knew him?'

'Oh, yes, we knew him. Is there no one else here? They must have a bigger staff than this, surely? Just a boss and a receptionist?'

'There's a little café just down the road. It serves this whole business estate. All the staff have been sent down there at Mr Bartholomew's expense. They were told to wait until they were called for. That seems to have been the other man's doing. As far as I can tell, he took charge. And we can be grateful, because one of the things he did was to make sure that no one touched anything. He assures me that this tableau is exactly as it was when he and Mr Bartholomew walked in here. And the receptionist didn't touch anything because, according to him, she had gone straight back into the car park and was running round and round, screaming.'

'So what can you tell us?'

'Right now? Very little. But that envelope the dead man is holding – I think that must have been placed there for a reason. Don't you? I've been waiting until you arrived to take a closer look at it.'

Susanna nodded. It always felt good, even when presented with a sight as foul as this one, to know that you were in the company of competent people. 'Thanks, Sally. Shall we open it?'

'I've already prepared the evidence bag and a label.' She removed the envelope from the dead man's hands so gently that she might have feared disturbing him. She was wearing gloves, but the person who put the envelope there might not have been, and so she handled it only by the edges. 'It isn't sealed. That's good, because it makes it easy to open. But it's unfortunate, because if the killer hasn't licked it we won't find any DNA in the gum.' She extracted a sheet of paper from the envelope and showed it to Susanna.

Your turn next,

Jensen Bartholomew

'He's a grammarian, at any rate,' said the CSM. 'He knows where to use a comma.' She put the sheet of paper and the envelope into the evidence bag, attached the label and sealed it.

'Thanks, Carol. I'll have a word with Jensen Bartholomew and his man and then I'll leave you to get on with it.' She walked across to where the three figures were sitting, Rayyan and Nicola following. Nicola had her tablet in her hand; as the junior of the three officers, taking notes would fall to her. All three showed their warrant cards, and Susanna gave their names. To the man beside Jensen, she said, 'I've already met Mr Bartholomew in the last twenty-four hours on a very similar matter. I don't think I've had the pleasure…?'

'Craig Murphy, Inspector. The agency I work for is providing Mr Bartholomew with personal protection. I drove him here this morning.'

'Indeed. And I believe it's you we have to thank for making sure no one interfered with the scene. Are you ex-Job?'

Murphy shook his head. 'Military police – we knew how to keep a scene inviolate.'

'And I'm grateful to you.' She turned to Bartholomew. 'Mr Bartholomew, the man in the chair. Have you ever seen him before?'

She was struck by how pale Bartholomew looked. He'd watched his own brother being murdered on screen only the day before, but to be presented with what he had seen this morning must have seemed even worse. 'No. Never. Craig asked me that and I've had plenty of time to think about it. I've no idea who he is. Or why anyone would have killed him in this building.'

'I can help you with that last question,' said Susanna. 'He was holding an envelope. Inside it was a message. The message says, "You're next, Jensen Bartholomew." So I have to ask you the same question you were asked yesterday. Can you think of any reason why someone who is killing other people should be threatening to kill you? And does it help if I tell you the man with his throat cut was known to us and went by the name of Ali Badaan?'

Bartholomew shook his head. 'Never heard of him. Sorry.'

Murphy said, 'If you know who he is, Inspector, should I assume Ali Badaan is known to the police, in the sense in which those words are usually used?'

'I'm sorry. I can't answer that.'

'I understand. I've already advised Mr Bartholomew that this building is a crime scene and your people are likely to want to keep possession of it for some time. I know how long SOCO investigations can take. He is able to work from home. If he sends all his people home for two days on full pay, is it likely they'll be able to come in again after that?'

'Possibly. I can't say for sure until the crime scene manager tells me what they have found.' She handed him her business card. 'Why don't you call me tomorrow afternoon and we'll see how we are getting on?'

'We'll do that.' He took the receptionist's hand in his. 'If we get you home, is there anyone there to be with you?'

45

'I think we'd prefer to take charge of that,' said Susanna. 'We'll take Miss…?'

'Brenda Hargreaves,' said Bartholomew.

'Thank you. We'll take Brenda to hospital and get her checked out. She's had a dreadful shock. We won't let her go home unless we are sure someone can be with her.'

* * *

When Rayyan and Nicola presented themselves once more at the entrance to Melody Fitzgerald's apartment block, the doorman told them to take a seat. 'I'll let Ms Fitzgerald know you're here. Someone else is with her at the moment.' Another ten minutes passed, and then the doors to the penthouse lift opened and out came *Post* reporter Bernadette Spence. She waved at the two officers. 'Melody says will you go straight up? She'll meet you at the top. Or, of course, you could save yourselves the time and just read my story when it comes out.' She laughed, and was gone.

Whatever images the name Melody Fitzgerald might have conjured up in Rayyan's mind, the reality was different. She was not particularly tall, not particularly slender, not particularly graceful and not particularly beautiful. And yet, there was about her an indefinable something – a sense that here was someone who could make you laugh and make you cry, and whichever she caused you to do would be intentional on her part. Rayyan was conscious that Nicola, who understood his susceptibility to women better than he did himself, was eyeing him with amusement. He straightened his own face – this was, after all, the ex-wife of a man who had just died. But Melody noticed the adjustment and commented on it. 'Can I just make something clear before we start? If you think you are calling on a grieving widow, you need to think again. I'm sorry for Cedric's sake that he's dead. But only for his sake. Would you like coffee, or shall we get straight to the point?'

Rayyan said, 'We'll dive straight in, shall we? Shall we all sit down?' When they had done that, he said, 'When did you marry Cedric Bartholomew? And when did you divorce him?'

'Eight years ago. Six years ago. Although we lived apart from three months after the wedding.'

'How did you meet him in the first place?'

'On a cruise ship. You could think of it as a floating casino; I dealt blackjack. Cedric bet big. He seemed like a good bet himself – a sure thing. Money no problem. We were engaged by the end of the cruise and the onboard chaplain married us.'

'Cedric swept you off your feet?'

Melody laughed. 'I don't think anyone's ever done that. I don't have that kind of feet. But I was tired of the cruise

47

ships, and he persuaded me – no, he didn't, I persuaded myself – that he would be a secure financial future. As it turned out, I was wrong. We divorced.'

'No children?' asked Nicola.

'That was never part of the agreement. You might have a child by a husband forty years older than you, if that's what it takes to seal the deal, because the husband will be dead before the child becomes an adult. It isn't something you do with a man younger than you.'

Rayyan's surprise was visible. 'You are older than Cedric?'

'That could have been more gracefully expressed. But, yes – I'll be forty next birthday, and Cedric will never now reach thirty-five.'

'Forgive me. You don't look it.'

'I work very hard not to look it. It becomes more difficult every year.'

Aware that he was out of his depth and not doing well, Rayyan looked towards Nicola to take up the questioning. She said, 'Melody, is Melody Fitzgerald your real name?'

'It's the name on my passport, my bank accounts, and my title to this apartment. Fitzgerald is an ancient name, you know. We are descended from those who came over with the Conqueror in 1066. If you want to get tied up in boring facts, Melody Fitzgerald is not what my mother called me. But facts can be modified for the greater good, and how would you like to go through the world saddled with the name Fanny O'Malley?'

Now it was Nicola's turn to laugh. She said, 'You live in circumstances very different from your ex-husband's. Would you mind telling us how you earn your living?'

'I have rich friends. They give me presents.'

'I see. And are these rich friends men? And are they the reason you need to work increasingly hard to look younger than you are?'

Watching this, Rayyan expected Melody to become angry, but it didn't happen. She said, 'You analyse my situation very well. The time may be drawing near to have that child by a father who will soon be dead. But those opportunities don't come up every day, and you have to be extremely careful. Men of that age with that kind of money tend to be pretty shrewd. They've seen most things and they expect value for money. I've seen too many girls end up chucked out and counting every penny three times before they spend it. That's the kind of valuable knowledge Bellerive didn't teach us.'

'Bellerive?' said Rayyan.

'A convent school in Liverpool. Run by the Faithful Companions of Jesus. There was a time the nuns thought I might have a vocation.'

Rayyan stared at her in silence. Nicola said, 'How do you and Jensen Bartholomew get along?'

'Well, *he* certainly won't be on my list of possible fathers. Not just because he's too young, but because I don't like him. He tried it on with me. Can you imagine that? Cedric brings me home after the cruise, introduces me as his wife, and his brother makes a pass. Lovely man.'

Nicola remembered what Jensen Bartholomew had said about the woman telling this story. Perhaps, in trying it on with Melody, he had been seeking to show his brother her true nature. And perhaps not everything Jensen Bartholomew had told them was true.

Rayyan said, 'Do you gain anything from Cedric Bartholomew's death?'

Now for the first time she did look a little annoyed. 'How? What? He didn't have a pot to piss in. He begged me for money several times. One of the things I'm most pleased about is that, when we married, I made sure he didn't know how much I had saved.'

'And do you know who killed him?'

She shook her head. 'I'm sorry he's dead. I know it probably doesn't look like that, and I don't mean I'll grieve for him because I won't. But he didn't deserve to die. Cedric was a pillock. He had very little in the way of brainpower, he was led by his dick in the way so many men are, and the idea of planning was completely foreign to him. But he didn't hurt people. If I could help you find who killed him, I would.'

'How did Cedric get on with his brother?'

'Badly. Cedric and Jensen both inherited money from their father. Jensen worked hard to multiply his. Cedric spent his share. Then he expected Jensen to treat him like the prodigal son. Kill the fatted calf. Jensen chose not to do that. I don't like him, but I can't say I blame him.'

Nicola said, 'Did you ever visit Cedric in Dryden Close?'

'Never.' Her eyes now were fixed on Rayyan's and he felt like a laboratory specimen under a microscope. 'When I'm with a man, I'm with him. Body and soul. And when it's over… It's over. Permanently and for ever. And that's how it was with me and Cedric.'

CHAPTER 5

A Widow Mourns

Bernadette Spence

When Melody Fitzgerald heard yesterday about the death of her one-time husband, Cedric Bartholomew, she was grief-stricken. 'Strictly speaking,' she said, 'I'm not really Cedric's widow. Cedric ended our marriage, for reasons I never understood. But I never stopped loving him.'

Speaking exclusively to The Post in her tastefully decorated penthouse suite overlooking the river, Melody poured out her heart. About the cruise on which they met. About the suddenness with which they realised the force of their feelings for each other. 'A whirlwind romance, you might call it,' said Melody. A whirlwind that ended in a ceremony in the cruise ship's chapel as they became man and wife. 'We became one,' said Melody. 'It says that in the service, but I never understood until Cedric and I were joined together how perfect an image that is.'

Melody can offer nothing to help the police. She has no idea why anyone would have wanted to hurt her ex, who she describes as a dear, innocent man. Nor can she suggest a reason why Cedric's brother, millionaire businessman Jensen Bartholomew, should have thought it necessary to hire a bodyguard. 'Neither of them was ever involved in anything underhand. I would stake my life on that.'

Police inquiries into what Melody calls "this senseless, pointless" killing continue.

* * *

The team in the incident room had grown in size, and there were more names on the board. Ali Badaan was one; the other was Yuri Malinov, nightwatchman. Blazeley said, 'None of us expected to be back here so quickly, but events make it necessary. Before we get to the two new deaths, does anyone have any development to report from the last briefing? Yes, Mahmoud. You have something for us?'

'The job centre was surprisingly cooperative. Cedric Bartholomew has been receiving six hundred and seventy pounds a month universal credit. His council tax was thirty-four pounds a week, but he only had to find seven pounds because the government subsidised him for the rest. The universal credit was paid into a bank account, because the government insists on that, and the bank was only as helpful as they had to be. Taffy got the feeling that they'd rather Bartholomew had gone somewhere else. He drew out the money in cash each month, only leaving one pound.'

'Date of last withdrawal?' Said Blazeley.

'Six days ago.'

'Well,' said Susanna. 'Six hundred and seventy pounds isn't a fortune, but it should have allowed him to live better than he did. There was no cash in the house and almost none in his pockets. So what was he doing with it?'

'We need to know,' said Blazeley. 'Marion, make sure that's on HOLMES. We need a full-scale examination of Cedric Bartholomew's life. Who did he see, where did he go, what did he spend his money on? Anyone else?'

Rayyan said, 'Nicola and I went back to see Melody Fitzgerald, whose mother thinks her daughter is called Fanny O'Malley. She's a good time girl.'

'She's a hooker,' said Nicola. 'Top of the line, and I don't doubt she gives value for money, but let's not dress up the oldest profession. She sells her body for money. When she sold it to Cedric Bartholomew, she thought it was a lifetime deal. The moment she realised her mistake, Cedric was out of her life. I'm not a man, but I suspect,' and she glanced at Rayyan, 'that when she's with them she makes men feel like they are the most important person in the world. But I don't think I've ever met anyone quite so ruthless.'

'I thought you liked her,' said Rayyan.

'I did,' said Nicola. 'You don't have to be a saint for me to like you. In fact, being a saint is probably a serious disadvantage. In any case, I don't think there's anything to tie her to Cedric's killing.'

Rayyan nodded. 'Agreed.'

'Who's next?' said Blazeley. When the crime scene manager for Cedric Bartholomew's murder put up his hand, he had a look of excitement he wasn't trying to suppress. 'Yes, Charlie,' said Blazeley. 'What have you got?'

'Prints,' said Charlie. 'Cedric Bartholomew's. I said we had them for elimination purposes, but in fact they turn out to be a little more than that. Six months ago, there was a break-in at a legal firm in the centre of town. A bunch of files were taken. One of the fingerprints found after the robbery was unknown. It isn't unknown now. It belonged to Cedric Bartholomew.'

'Well,' said Blazeley. 'What was that about? Marion, I don't suppose it was the major crime team that investigated that break-in. Find out who it was, and assign Theresa to talk to them. Theresa, next briefing, come back to us with everything there is to know about the files that were taken and any possible connection with Bartholomew. What's next, Marion?'

Nicola said, 'I think I am. I was looking into the numbers on the victim's phone. Who he called, and who called him.'

'What have you found out?'

'Nothing – at least as far as the calls are concerned. The only identifiable number is his brother's. Apart from that, anyone he called and anyone who called him was using a burner phone.'

Susanna said, 'And that in itself is suspicious. Who uses burner phones? Criminals. They buy a phone…'

'… Or they steal one,' said Nicola. 'Three of the phones on the list were using stolen SIM cards. Which does rather reinforce the criminal aspect. And so does the fact that I rang each of the numbers, and they were all dead.'

Blazeley said, 'Which suggests that whoever owned those phones knew Cedric was dead, knew we'd be investigating who his contacts were, and didn't want to be identified so they got rid of the phone. So we can be pretty certain that Cedric Bartholomew was mixed up in some criminal business. Especially when you add to those burner phones the fingerprint at an office break-in.'

Nicola said, 'I said I found nothing as far as the calls were concerned. But what the telecoms unit hadn't had time to check when we first got the list of numbers was the location monitoring.' She put a map against the transparent plastic board that names and photos were already fixed to. 'This is a map of the places the phone company says that phone has been in the last week.' She put another map beside the first. 'And this is where it's been in the last three months, with dates. I say this is where the phone has been and not this is where Cedric has been, because we don't know that it was always in his possession. It seems a reasonable bet, though.'

'Good work, Nicola,' said Blazeley. 'It's a pity the phone is only three months old – we won't be able to place it at the office break-in six months ago. Right. We have two new murders to deal with, and the note that was left at the last one means we can be certain that they are connected with the killing of Cedric Bartholomew. Let's talk about what we have so far. First, Ali Badaan. He's quite well known to people in this building, but not to major crime, so I've asked Hamed here to tell us about him. Hamed?'

Hamed was a detective sergeant who'd been on the force for a number of years and never expressed any interest in moving to major crime. He stepped into the space in front of Blazeley. 'Ali Badaan is indeed an old friend of ours. He's a Batterton native. Born here and educated here. And it was a good education; his teachers had great hopes for him. Potentially a mathematician, an electronics engineer, or an IT guru. None of that worked out, for reasons I can't tell you because I don't know, and he's lived on the wrong side of the law for a number of years. If you wanted someone to bypass sophisticated alarm systems so that you could enter somewhere you shouldn't, Ali was your man. He was sentenced for it twice. Suspended both times. I sometimes wonder which side judges are on.'

'Someone like that,' said Blazeley, 'needs someone finding him work.'

'Terry Winkleman,' said Hamed. 'He's very well connected, fingers in many pies, been arrested three times, it never got as far as a courtroom because we could never persuade the Crown Prosecution Service we had the evidence to get a conviction. He lives in a house by the river, just outside the park. You must have seen it – pink walls to the house and a purple garage with a Chevy Impala parked outside it. The Impala almost never goes anywhere. It's quite ancient and it's there for show. Terry has a white Ford van he uses for most things; his wife drives a bright red Honda Civic. I've no doubt you'll talk to him; if you get anything, you'll be a step up on us because he's never told us a damn thing.'

Blazeley said, 'Marion, an action for HOLMES. Rayyan to visit Mr Winkleman and ask his assistance. Take a DC with you, Rayyan. Thanks, Hamed – that's been very useful. The other victim was Yuri Malinov. He was the night watchman and he died from head injuries after being hit over the head with something very heavy. Professor Baines found fibres in the wound which suggest that the murder weapon was wrapped in a grey woollen sock. We're hopeful of getting DNA from the fibres.'

Hamed said, 'I think you can assume that the DNA won't belong to Ali Badaan. We've never even suspected him of violence and I don't really think he's capable of it. Not big enough, not strong enough, and really not nasty enough. The last job we got him for, someone else had gone in first and sidelined the nightwatchman and then Ali had done his part of the job. That may well be what happened here. I don't suppose killing the watchman was intentional. Most likely, he was hit too hard.'

'So,' said Blazeley, 'as a working hypothesis, we have this. Someone – quite possibly Terry Winkleman – organised someone else to go in and whack Yuri Malinov to make it possible for Ali Badaan to disable the alarm system. What we don't know is who asked Winkleman, and presumably paid him, to make those arrangements. Nor do we know why. It seems that nothing was stolen, and nothing damaged, so the assumption must be that the only reason for choosing that building was to make Jensen Bartholomew aware of the threat against him.'

Susanna said, 'That does sound likely, boss. Even so, we'll still need to talk to any family Yuri Malinov might have had, and anyone who knew him.'

'We certainly will,' said Blazeley. 'I was offering one hypothesis. There are others.'

'And,' said Rayyan, 'is the threat serious?'

'I understand why you ask the question,' said Blazeley. 'The result of threatening Jensen Bartholomew has been to make him harder to attack, because he now has a professional minder. So is the killer really trying to put the frighteners on him? Or is there some other objective?'

Rayyan said, 'The killer may just be not very bright.'

'True,' said Blazeley. 'Well, as always, let's keep an open mind till we know more.'

CHAPTER 6

Harold Frobisher knew that, when his wife got home from her constituents' surgery as an MP, she expected to be told what connection might exist between her, her husband and the late and sadly unlamented Cedric Bartholomew. And Harold would have liked to comply. He couldn't, because he didn't know the answers. But he knew someone who did.

He rang Jensen Bartholomew's office and found his call automatically rerouted to Bartholomew's mobile. 'Jensen? Harold Frobisher. Where are you?'

'I'm at home. The office building is a crime scene. No one's allowed in without a white paper suit and a mask. That look doesn't suit me.'

'Okay. I need to talk to you about something your brother did for Jenny. Can I come round?'

There was a short pause and then Bartholomew said, 'It isn't for me to say, Harold. I have a bodyguard and he vets anyone coming near me. You'd need his approval.'

'A bodyguard? Why do you need a bodyguard?'

'You have read this morning's *Post*?'

'I… Yes.'

'Then you know I have a bodyguard. His name is Craig Murphy. He's an ex-cop. I watched my brother being murdered, Harold. What the *Post* didn't tell you is that the killer told me I'd be next. If you want to come here, you need to talk to Craig and tell him why. If he says it's okay, sure – come over. In fact, you can bring me some cigarettes.'

'You don't smoke.'

'Not for years,' agreed Bartholomew. 'I'm under pressure. I feel like starting again.'

Harold Frobisher was nobody's fool. You couldn't be, and get away with what he had got away with over the years – as a councillor, a businessman, and his wife's political agent. He knew that in the whole barrage of words he'd just been subjected to, the ones that mattered were, "He's an ex-cop." Jensen wouldn't want the kind of conversation they needed to have to be conducted in front of someone who might still have police connections. And nor did Harold. But they couldn't talk on the phone, because who knew who might be listening in? He said, 'It wasn't that urgent. Let me know when you're back in circulation. And lay off the fags, Jensen. They'll kill you as surely as this unknown moron killed Cedric.'

And, as it happened, it really didn't matter that he hadn't been able to speak to Bartholomew because when Jenny got home, tired and fractious after spending time with constituents for whom she felt little but contempt, she had changed her mind. She held up a hand when Harold raised the subject. 'It has the feel of one of those stories that run and run when the Press get hold of them and do you no good at all. I want to be able to deny any knowledge. So don't tell me. And I have no patience for cooking this evening, so unless you want to go into the kitchen yourself we'll eat out or we'll get something delivered. You choose; I need a shower.'

Harold rang the nearest thing Batterton had to a Michelin starred restaurant. Left to himself, he'd have preferred to get the local Indian to send in an assortment of dishes but, when an MP lived with you, you had to be careful. It wouldn't be the first time he found some hack going through their dustbins looking for something they could make a story out of. You had to hand it to Jenny – she knew as much as he did about the job Cedric Bartholomew had done for them, because she had told him to make the arrangements. But, as she'd told him before, he had less far to fall than she did and was therefore more disposable. Her dreams of a cabinet post had not yet born fruit, but Jenny was not one to give up.

* * *

Bernadette Spence and *The Post's* editor sat in the editor's office and watched the television as a tearful Melody Fitzgerald poured out her heart to watching millions as she had earlier poured it out to Bernadette. 'You've got to give it to her,' said Bernie. 'She's a real pro. She even had the foresight to remove her mascara before the tears came.'

The editor nodded. 'It's one of the best sales videos I've ever seen.'

'You think that's what it is? You think she's selling herself?'

'To the highest bidder. She's offering the goods. "This body can be yours. If you have the asking price. And you can count on me to keep my trap shut." I wonder what she knows.'

'What do you mean?'

'Come on, Bernie,' said the editor. 'You know better than that. What's her target market?'

'Well. Wealthy businessmen. *Older* wealthy businessmen.'

'Precisely. And how did those older businessmen become wealthy? They fiddled the books. They cheated the taxman. They charged VAT, but didn't hand it over. They traded in illegal goods. Counterfeit goods. Goods produced in ways your average *Guardian* reader wouldn't approve of. And then, when they'd made their pile, they turned legit. And what they need most of all in any woman they pick to comfort them as they sail towards the oblivion that awaits us all is that she keeps their secrets. Remains silent. Says nothing to anyone, and especially to reporters and the police. And that's how she's setting out her stall. She did it in her interview with you and we've just seen her do it again on television. "Whatever I know, I tell no one. Even when the marriage is over. You can trust me." It was a great performance. I hope it works for her.'

'Well, you old cynic.'

'I'm a newspaper editor, Bernie. That's the definition of a cynic.'

'If you're right, I wonder what it is she does know.'

'Something about Cedric and his brother, for starters. But she'll never tell you.'

* * *

DC Theresa Pearson regretted the closure of the police canteen. They'd been warned that the drive to save money meant costs had to be cut somewhere and they'd been promised consultation – but consultation had turned out to mean what it usually meant; a decision had been made, the people it affected most had been invited to say what they thought, and then the decision had been carried out unmodified. There was other stuff going on – staggered refreshment breaks were already in effect and a move to single-officer cars was being threatened. Neither of those things applied to Theresa, because detective's meal breaks had always been staggered – you took one when you could, often with no idea when you'd have another opportunity – and because she no longer drove a police car. But Jamie, her husband, did, and she worried on his behalf. Leaving aside the job satisfaction she knew Jamie got from mentoring younger officers as he had once mentored her, driving around in a police car was sometimes very dangerous. She remembered what was probably the last time danger had come to her and Jamie. They'd been called to a break-in at a jewellery store. The owner had been knifed and the robber had tried very hard to do the same to her. If Jamie had not been there… She didn't like to think about it.

And the other problem with the absence of a canteen was that there was nowhere that she and Jamie could arrange to meet for a cup of tea and a plate of saturated fats. That was going to matter more than usual over the coming days and nights because a murder investigation meant that members of the Major Crime Investigation Team didn't get home much except to shower, sleep and change their clothes.

If it came to that, she regretted the loss of a place where team members could get together and shoot the breeze about their day. Regular twice-daily briefings meant they were up-to-date with everything that was going on, but that wasn't the same as being able to kick ideas around and reduce the pressures of a hard job just by talking about it. She'd heard it suggested that more officers now had mental health problems and that the reason was that they'd lost the place where other officers could ask how they were doing. Where they could talk about marital pressures, job stress and trouble with the kids and be offered sympathy and support.

Well, there was no point complaining about it. The decision to close the canteen had been made by someone on a pay grade so far above hers it was almost unimaginable. A canteen would have been a very good place to talk to the officers who had investigated the theft of files from a law firm. But there wasn't one, and so she was perched on the edge of DC Samantha Piretti's desk because there were no chairs that didn't already have someone's backside in them.

Samantha said, 'I had to go back into NICHE to remember. It wasn't so long ago, but you know how it is… Every detective has too many cases and if you don't watch out, they blur. Anyway. This is what I can tell you. We got a call from Patel and Mayfield. You know them?' When Theresa shook her head, Samantha went on, 'No reason why you should. The only criminal cases they do are pro bono defence jobs. Their main business is immigration cases. So, they called and said they'd had a break in. They knew they'd had one, because they have a state-of-the-art alarm system and it was switched off. Okay, you say; maybe someone forgot to turn it on. But they hadn't, because the CCTV had recorded Patel herself doing it when she left the office at seven the previous evening. Right, you think – they have CCTV. So let's have a look at the bit that shows someone interfering with the alarm. But we couldn't, because that part of the recording had been deleted. When we asked what had been stolen, they said: Almost nothing. Expensive IT equipment untouched. A phone left where it had been charging. There had been fifty quid in the petty cash box and that was gone, but they couldn't see that anything else was missing. SOCO went over the place, naturally, and the only thing they found was a single fingerprint on the cash box. We might have thought it was kids – they took the money but they left everything else because they wouldn't know how to get rid of it and they might not even have been able to carry it. But it wasn't kids. Not with that level of know-how in turning off the alarm and deleting the CCTV. The fingerprint wasn't on file. It certainly wasn't Ali Badaan's, because that was the first thing we checked. If he hadn't done it, it must have been someone from out of town because no one around else here has that level of expertise.'

'You questioned him?'

'Oh, yes, we questioned him. The interviews will still be on file. You can take a look at them. They'll tell you exactly as much as they told us. Bugger all. So we were ready to leave it. I mean, fifty pounds stolen and no damage done – how can you justify doing anything with the kind of workload we have and the number of people available to do it? But then we got another call, a few days later. They'd only just noticed that three files had disappeared. Must have gone at the time of the break-in because there hadn't been another one. We didn't get a great deal of sense out of the Patel woman about what the files were, except that they were important. She said it was confidential. The Sarge said nothing was confidential when you're talking to the police, and she gave him one of those prissy looks lawyers do and said she thought she understood the law better than he did. "Better than any policeman," was what she actually said. You can imagine how keen the Sarge was to go on digging after that.'

'Right,' said Theresa. 'If I want to know any more, I guess I need to talk to Miss Patel.'

'I guess you do. And if you don't want to get off to the worst possible start, I suggest you make that Ms Patel.'

Theresa went back to the incident room and told Susanna what had happened. 'Somebody needs to go and talk to Lawyer Patel.' She turned to Marion. 'Is there an action on HOLMES assigned to me?'

'If there is,' said Susanna, 'it can wait. You've got the story so far, so you can do the Patel and Mayfield visit. Find Rayyan and get him to go with you.'

* * *

The first thing Bernadette Spence did when the editor handed her the police press release on the deaths of Ali Badaan and Yuri Malinov was to search *The Post*'s archive looking for both names. Yuri Malinov wasn't mentioned anywhere, but she soon had an understanding of how Ali Badaan had made his living. The press release wasn't exactly informative. They never were. All it said was that the two men had died at business premises owned by Jensen Bartholomew's company and that police regarded the deaths as suspicious. Bernie was prepared to bet that she knew what Ali had been there for – he had been opening the place up for someone else's nefarious intent. According to the archive, that was what he did, and the archive was a lot more forthcoming than a police press release. But who had killed him? Had whoever it was also killed the other man? And what was the other man doing there? With a name like that, he was probably an East European migrant. Had he been sleeping rough, woken up to see a murder in process and been silenced? She needed to know. She was pretty sure, after she'd tried to interview him when his brother was killed, that Jensen Bartholomew wasn't going to tell her anything. If she wanted more from the police, she'd have to wait for a press conference, when every other journo would have access to the same information at the same time and when, in any case, the police might still not be terribly forthcoming. Fortunately, there were other ways to skin this cat.

She logged into Facebook and searched for the name of Jensen Bartholomew's company. It came up attached to three pages. One belonged to the company itself and she scanned that just to see what it said.

Business as usual

You may have heard of the unpleasant goings-on at our Batterton office, which appear to have been a random incident that had nothing to do with us except that the perpetrators chose our premises. It could have happened anywhere; it happened to happen here. The building is at present a crime scene, but rest assured that we continue in business. Phone or email us in the usual way and in the usual way is how we will get back to you.

As with the police press release, no hard information there. She moved on to the first of the other two pages. This was in the name of someone who worked for the company. It made no reference at all to anything unusual having happened and the reason was clear when Bernie looked at the photographs that had been posted only yesterday. The page owner was on holiday in Gran Canaria. It was on the third and final page that she struck gold. Sheila Hegarty, the page owner, also worked there and had posted a breathless account of what she had seen when she turned up for work. Bernie sent her a private message introducing herself, saying readers of *The Post* would love to hear Sheila's story in her own words, and asking for a meeting.

While she waited for a reply, Bernie did a quick search of the electoral register and found an address for Yuri Malinov. Not a rough sleeper, then. If he'd lived alone, that would have been that – but he hadn't. Katarina Malinov was registered at the same address, which Bernie jotted down before turning back to Facebook. Sheila Hegarty must have been online, because the reply was immediate. Yes, she would love to give *The Post*'s readers an insight into what had happened. Another quick exchange of messages and Bernie had Sheila's address. "On my way," she messaged and received a thumbs-up emoji by return. She told the editor, 'I'll be back as quick as I can. I should have the lowdown on these killings, so save me some space.'

* * *

It took Theresa some time to catch up with Rayyan, and the sergeant groaned just a little when she told him what they were to do. 'I've heard about this Patel woman. She switches between patronising and insulting. Honestly, Theresa, it's a common thing with lawyers. They look down on the police. Well, let's get it over with.'

But that was just what they couldn't do. When they arrived, the receptionist told them that Ms Patel was out of the office for the rest of the day. 'How about Ms Mayfield?' asked Rayyan.

'She's at an immigration tribunal. We don't expect her back till tomorrow.'

'We are here about some files that you reported stolen some months ago. Is there anyone else who can help us?'

The receptionist shook her head. 'We don't have any other lawyers, and right now we don't have any interns. It's a small practice. Just the two partners and me. And I wouldn't be prepared to talk to the police.'

'Prepared? Or competent?'

'I don't know enough about the subject. I know files disappeared, but I have no idea which files they were. Surely, your officers must have found out when they investigated?'

Rayyan looked at Theresa, who shook her head. 'Ms Patel wasn't prepared to say.'

'They can't have been very important then,' said Rayyan. He handed the receptionist his card. 'This is a murder investigation.'

The receptionist's hand had gone to her mouth. 'Murder? But…'

'Yes, murder. And the one thing we can be certain of in a murder investigation is that we won't have enough time. For anything. Which means we can't keep popping in here on the off chance that one of the partners will be able to see us. Please ask Ms Patel to call me when she is sure she'll be able to give us at least thirty minutes of her time.'

CHAPTER 7

Sheila Hegarty was watching through the window as Bernie Spence got out of the car. The reporter was used to that; she was often able to get information denied to the police because people loved talking to the press. They loved talking on television even more and for a while she'd dreamed about a job in TV but she'd been disabused of that idea before she'd even left college. 'It's a cruel world,' a lecturer had told her. 'A man can appear on the box and no one cares what he looks like, but I'm afraid higher standards are set for the appearance of women TV journos. Better stick to the print, Bernadette. You have what it takes to make it all the way to the Street of Shame and beyond.'

And Bernie, who didn't have any inflated opinion of her own appearance and who had already learned from experience that a man's glance tended to pass on to another as soon as it alighted on her, accepted that. Fleet Street was her aim – a symbolic aim now that none of the big circulation papers was any longer based there. She wondered sometimes whether there was anything she wouldn't do to get there. She thought there probably wasn't.

She was shown into a cramped, untidy room. 'Please excuse the mess,' said Sheila Hegarty. 'I live here alone and since yesterday I haven't felt like tidying up. Can I get you a coffee?'

'I'll come with you.' Bernie wasn't sure that she wanted anything to eat or drink in a place as unkempt as this, but she knew that accepting was the right thing to do. Refusing placed a barrier between them. She did not, after all, need to drink it. And her fears eased when they reached the kitchen, which was spotless and looked after. The glass tabletop looked polished and clean; there were no dirty dishes, in the sink or elsewhere; the atmosphere was one of a place for everything and everything in its place.

'It's just instant, I'm afraid,' said Sheila and Bernie wondered why that sentence was spoken so often. Most coffee drunk in this country was instant, and most of it was fine. In fact, Bernie sometimes wondered about the mentality of people who were hung up on the right kind of grinder, the right kind of machine and the right kind of beans. Coffee was coffee. They sat at the kitchen table, and Bernie accepted with pleasure a clean plate and a Danish pastry. She placed her digital recorder on the table and pressed the Record button. 'So,' she said. 'Tell me all about it.' And they were off – the effect was like the start of the Grand National.

76

'It was terrible!' But Sheila's face bore an expression of glee. 'I was the second to arrive. Brenda – that's Brenda Hargreaves, the receptionist – was running around the car park, screaming her head off. She was crying her eyes out and I wouldn't be a bit surprised if you told me she'd wet herself. I slapped her face.'

'What?'

'That's what they taught us. In the Guides. For the first aid badge. If someone is in a state of panic, you speak to them very sharply and slap them. You know – to calm them down. I said, "Brenda! Pull yourself together! What's the matter with you?" And she – she just pointed towards the door. She didn't seem capable of speaking. So, I went where she was pointing. It was like something out of Madame Tussauds. You know – a waxwork. A Bloody Murders exhibit. This man, sitting in a chair, staring at me. Well, obviously, he wasn't really staring because he was dead and you have to be alive to stare. But that's how it seemed. As if he was looking at me. Looking straight into my eyes. And *his* eyes – they were big. As though he'd just had the most amazing surprise. Which, I suppose, he must have had. Blood had soaked down from his throat onto… Well, it was a rather nice jacket he was wearing. Blue and white stripes.'

'You must have been looking at him for quite a long time.'

Sheila's eyes went as large as the ones she'd just been describing. 'I couldn't look away! It was mesmerising. I'm an office worker. I've never seen a dead body before. Not even my parents – my brother looked after all that when they went. And I'd certainly never seen someone whose throat had been cut.'

'You think that's how he died?'

'Sure of it. You could tell. From his chin upwards, he looked fine. Except for the surprised look I've told you about. Immediately below his chin it was red. Dark red. You think of blood as being brighter than that. But it wasn't, it was dark. And it was dark on his nice jacket, too.'

'That's tremendous material, Sheila. Thank you so much. Is there anything else you can remember about the dead man?'

'He had an envelope. The whole thing looked posed to me. Like he'd been sat there after he was dead and his arms had been arranged so that his hands came together and between them – like he was holding it out for someone – this envelope.'

'You make a marvellous witness. Have the police talked to you about it yet?'

'I had a phone call saying they'd be here this afternoon. I suppose they must have an awful lot to do.'

A burst of warmth passed through Bernie. Not only had she beaten the cops, but she was going to have time to file her story before they ever got here. She said, 'It's interesting that they chose that building to leave the body in. What can you tell me about the company's business?'

'Well… What do you want to know? We're an import export company. We bring things into the country and we send things out.'

'What sort of things?'

'All sorts. Whatever people want. And we get stuff made for people. Somebody has a design, they want a company in China to make it because it will be cheaper, but they don't know how to go about it. Mr Bartholomew does. And he is very ecologically aware. We used to handle a lot of teak, but the forests aren't managed very well and Mr Bartholomew was pretty sure the certificates that came with it were often faked. So he went down to Australia and New Zealand and found hard timbers down there as a substitute. Kwila, for example – I'd never heard of it, but it's just excellent if you're looking for decking. It lasts forever and nothing bores into it. And it costs a lot less than teak. All that sort of stuff, I look after. Mr Bartholomew does the travelling, he makes the deals, and then it's over to me. I mean, I'm not suggesting… Mr Bartholomew does a lot of work on his own. He has customers and suppliers who he's had for ever and he looks after them personally. His brother, Mr Cedric, he had one or two, but Mr Bartholomew looks after them since Mr Cedric retired from the business.'

'What kind of customers and suppliers does Mr Bartholomew look after himself?'

'Well, that's just it. I don't know – I don't deal with them. Mr Bartholomew does everything, even including the invoicing. Those are customers he inherited from his father – but that was long before my time.'

Bernie turned off the recorder and placed a business card on the table. 'You've been enormously helpful, Sheila. I'm going to go now and write my story. If you think of anything else, call me.' She stood up. 'And thank you for the coffee and the pastry. Just what I needed.'

She looked at her watch. Just enough time to get to the address she had for Yuri Malinov, talk to his widow and get back to file her story before the afternoon deadline. She found to her delight that the editor was out at lunch with an advertiser. His deputy had never been able to resist Bernie's demands. She beefed up the story way beyond what she had intended and the deputy editor crossed her fingers and okayed it.

Did Killer Leave a Message?

Bernadette Spence

Sheila Hegarty, the first person to see Ali Badaan close-up after he had been killed, raises interesting questions. 'He was sitting there as though he'd been posed. His arms had been arranged so that his hands came together. They held an envelope. It looked like he was holding it out to someone.' Of course, Sheila had the good sense not to touch anything and so she wasn't able to say what was in the envelope. The police will know, but so far they aren't saying. But Sheila isn't in any doubt. 'It was a message. Obviously. I don't know who it was to, I don't know who it was from, though I assume it was the killer, and I don't know what it said. But it was a message. We can be sure of that.'

Ali Badaan has appeared in these pages before. When he was growing up in Batterton, his teachers forecast a future as an electronics engineer. And his teachers were right. Unfortunately, Ali chose to exercise his talents on the wrong side of the law. He has twice been sentenced to periods in jail for using his skills to bypass sophisticated alarm systems as part of the execution of a burglary. Both of those sentences were

*suspended, and friends of Ali wonder
whether, if he'd actually had to serve his
time, he might have changed his ways and
avoided his bloody death.*

*Sheila Hegarty isn't in any doubt about how
Ali died. 'His throat was cut from ear to
ear. He was wearing a really nice blue and
white jacket, and it was quite ruined by
being soaked in his blood.'*

*Questions must be asked about the choice of
Batterton millionaire businessman Jensen
Bartholomew's business empire as the site of
this brutal murder. Was he, in fact, the
person the murderer's message was addressed
to? Was Ali Badaan there to open up the
premises for someone? Did he misjudge his
paymaster? And what was in that building
that intruders wanted?*

*Sheila Hegarty could think of nothing in the
Bartholomew business that might have
provoked a killing. 'We bring things into the
country and we send things out. Ordinary
things. The sort of things everybody needs.'
While Jensen Bartholomew deals personally*

with some suppliers and some customers, she is sure nothing is untoward.

Concern over the death of Ali Badaan should not blind us to the tragedy that another man died at the same time and in the same place. Nightwatchman Yuri Malinov was killed by a savage blow to the head. His widow, Katarina Malinov, was inconsolable today. 'We came to this country for a better life. We would make whatever sacrifices we had to. In Slovenia I was a certificated English teacher and Yuri was a chemical engineering graduate, but here I worked as a carer and a cleaner and Yuri was a watchman at night and worked four hours every afternoon as a gardener. We were ready to do that because when we had saved enough money we planned to have children and we thought they would have a more secure future here.'

That more secure future, and the possibility of starting a family, have been ripped away. Katarina does not know what she will do now, but says she will almost certainly return to Slovenia.

Within ten minutes of that story appearing, the editor of *The Post* received a call demanding he present himself at the police station without delay and ask for Detective Superintendent McAvoy. When he returned an hour later, he called Bernie Spence and the deputy editor to his office for a dressing down.

'The murders of Ali Badaan and Yuri Malinov are *sub judice*. We are allowed to report that they are dead and that the police have not ruled out the possibility that the deaths may be suspicious. And that is all. You two both know that. So what the hell did you think you were doing?'

Bernie said, 'Boss, you know nobody takes any notice of *sub judice* rules any more.'

'I don't know that, Bernadette. What I know is that the police take those rules very seriously and that the person in the firing line is the editor. Me. You wrote the story, and you,' he said, turning towards the deputy editor, 'approved it for publication but the person who can go to jail is me. As a detective superintendent has just reminded me. The police are more pissed off than I can give voice to. As I am myself. You, Bernie, will not, now or at any time in the future, attempt to bypass me in the approve for publication process. If you do, you'll be gone. And you,' looking once more at the deputy editor, 'are clearly not up to the job. Sit at your desk and wait to hear from HR. I shall be asking them to suspend you while your conduct is investigated. I'll make it clear that, when the investigation is over, I don't expect you to return to work for this paper. Now get out of my sight, the pair of you.'

Hamed's description of Terry Winkleman's house made it easy for Rayyan and Nicola to find. The Chevy Impala was parked outside the purple garage, but so was a white Ford van. There was no sign of the bright red Honda Civic that Hamed had said belonged to Winkleman's wife.

When they rang the doorbell, it was answered without haste but with no delay. They introduced themselves, and Winkleman smiled a private smile as he showed them into a sitting room furnished at considerable expense and with no little taste. Winkleman sat down and invited his visitors to do the same. 'What can the police possibly want with me?'

Rayyan said, 'Ali Badaan was murdered sometime last night.'

'Ali Badaan? I'm sorry, I don't think I know the name. Who was he?'

They had talked on the way here about how to play this conversation. There was clearly no point in simply challenging Winkleman – that had been tried before. If they had firm evidence of contact between him and Ali Badaan, they could arrest him which would give them the right to interview him under caution, take his fingerprints and DNA, and search his home and any other premises they found him to be connected with. But they hadn't. There had never been enough evidence to persuade a senior officer to authorise Winkleman's arrest, and there wasn't now. The phone companies had come up with one possible link, but it contained more holes than a colander. They agreed that all they really had was an opportunity to appeal to his sense of self-preservation. Rayyan said, 'Mr Winkleman. I know you've had conversations like this with other officers in the past, and I know that you've never felt able to respond.'

Winkleman said, 'If I haven't responded, it's because I had nothing to say. It's true that I've had the conversations, though I've never understood why. I have no connection with any criminal elements whatsoever. Sadly, the police don't seem to believe that. I can only assume that someone in the past said something bad about me in order to cover up for someone else.'

'I hear what you say,' said Rayyan. 'What I'm suggesting now is that the stakes are so high that you might want to be a little more open. In case what happened to Ali Badaan happens to you.'

Rayyan knew that Winkleman's smile was intended to irritate him and he didn't plan to let that happen.

Winkleman said, 'Didn't you say this man had been murdered? Are you suggesting that someone might want to murder me? Why?'

As they had planned, Nicola stepped in. 'Mr Winkleman, it's been suggested to us by sources we trust that you act as a middleman in criminal activity.' Winkleman's smile had grown broader, but Nicola pressed on. 'Our sources tell us that you receive requests for something to be done – a nightwatchman to be sidelined, an alarm to be bypassed, a stolen getaway vehicle to be in place – and you pass on those requests to people able and prepared to carry them out.'

Winkleman said, 'Is that what this Ali Badaan person you mention did? Was he a nightwatchman? Did he steal cars? Was he good with alarms? Those aren't activities I know anything about, so forgive me if I'm unable to help.'

'The thing is, Mr Winkleman, a phone call was made to Ali Badaan just a few hours before he was murdered. We believe that was the phone call that gave him the instructions for the job on which he was killed.'

'Yes?'

'And that call, Mr Winkleman, was made from somewhere very close to this house.'

Winkleman spread out his arms as if indicating the geography of the place. 'We are right on the river. A towpath runs past the end of our garden. People walk up and down there all day long. On the other side of our garden fence is a park. Have you any idea how many people use that park?' He took a mobile phone from his pocket and passed it to Nicola. 'But see for yourself. Go through the list of people I've called. You won't find this Ali person's number there.'

Rayyan and Nicola exchanged a glance. They hadn't really expected to get anywhere, and they weren't going to. Rayyan said, 'There's a killer around. The most brutal, savage killer this town has seen since long before I became a policeman. I'm sorry that we can't persuade you to protect yourself.'

Winkleman's smile now had a different quality. 'Oh,' he said. 'Don't you worry about me, officer. I won't come to any harm.'

Always game for one last try, Rayyan said, 'Mr Winkleman. When people say things like that, they often mean that they have prepared a security mechanism. Usually, they've left a record somewhere that will incriminate someone and will be released if anything happens to them. That's fine, as long as whoever you're dealing with is capable of rational thought. It seems to me that the man who murdered Cedric Bartholomew and has now killed Ali Badaan and Yuri Malinov is a stranger to sanity. Are you sure you want to take that chance?'

Winkleman winked at Nicola and stood up. 'Will that be all?'

As Rayyan and Nicola left, a red Honda Civic was driving in. Winkleman's wife got out of it and watched the detectives leave. She said, 'They look like police to me. What did they want?'

Winkleman shook his head. 'Something very unpleasant is going on in this town. They think I'm involved, but it's way above my level. I've had nothing to do with it and I plan to keep it that way. It's a bastard, though – Ali Badaan has been killed. God knows where I'll find someone else with his talents.'

CHAPTER 8

Nicola's phone buzzed with the sound that signalled a text message. The name on the screen was her sister's. "Where are you right now? Can you speak?"

Nicola pressed the "Call Back" button. 'I'm on my way to the station. Be there in twenty minutes. But, honestly, Sasha, I don't have time to talk. We've got three murders on the go.'

'I know that, Nic. I do read the papers. I'm bringing you something to eat. I can't solve your murders, but I can make sure you keep body and soul together.'

Nicola felt a surge of warmth towards her sister. Sasha was the younger sister but, even as children, Sasha had always taken care of Nicola and not the other way round. She said, 'You're a star. I'll wait for you by the door.'

But there was no need for that because, when Nicola and Rayyan pulled into the police station car park, Sasha was already there. She handed over an insulated bag. 'Let me have this back when you're done with it. Don't bother washing anything – you don't have time for that and we have a dishwasher.' She kissed Nicola on the cheek. 'And don't put yourself in danger.' And then she was gone.

When Nicola unzipped the bag in the incident room, she could feel the envy of those around her. The standard fare for detectives hunting a murderer was chips and anything that went with them. Sasha had brought Nicola an insulated jug of hot mushroom soup and a bowl to drink it from, some buttered cheesy rolls and cooked chicken pieces that radiated aromas of sage, tarragon and oregano, and some sticky toffee pudding. Seeing the look on Rayyan's face, she placed two rolls and two pieces of chicken on one of the linen napkins Sasha had put into the bag and pushed them across the table. 'There's too much for me. Help me out.'

As he tucked in, Rayyan said, 'Your sister must be a hell of a cook.'

'Oh, I don't suppose she made this herself. Sasha's husband makes a great deal of money, and Sasha knows how to spend it.'

'Did you ever go out with that George Clooney lookalike she set you up with?'

'You've got a good memory. That was… When was that?'

'It was while we were looking for the two female serial killers. Your sister had arranged for you to meet this guy at a dinner party, but we were too busy with the case.'

'It wasn't really Sasha's idea – she did it to stop our mother nagging. But, yes, I did meet him afterwards. Just the once. To keep our mother quiet.'

'Your mother doesn't like you being single?'

'She doesn't like me being in the police. And she doesn't like me not giving her grandchildren that she can boast about. Being able to boast is important to her. She was mortified when I became a cop. And it was even worse when she realised I was going to have to start in uniform. Suppose one of her friends saw me!'

'It must be difficult to have a pushy mother.'

'I can't tell you how difficult. When I was six, our father got me involved in martial arts.'

'Oh, yes,' said Rayyan. 'I heard you were pretty good.'

'At first, our mother thought it was shocking. A girl – fighting. When Sasha came along a couple of years later, mother put her foot down – Sasha wasn't going anywhere near martial arts. But then, when she realised I was good...'

'Exceptional was the word I heard.'

'Yes, well – when one of the instructors told her I could end up an Olympic gold medallist, she completely changed her tune. You'd have thought she was the one who put me in for it in the first place. And then, when I decided that level of dedication wasn't for me, it was as though I had deliberately set out to spite her.'

'Why did you decide that?'

'I wanted to do other things. Lead a normal life. Have other interests. You can't do both. If Olympic gold is your aim, you have to forget about everything else. I wasn't ready to do that.'

'This guy… Did he really look like George Clooney?'

'I suppose he did, a bit. But that didn't do him any favours as far as I was concerned. Don't you think people like George Clooney are a bit up themselves? Always setting an example for the rest of us? And making sure we all know about it? Anyway… This guy… He's made a name for himself as an international finance journalist.'

'Exciting.'

'Yeah. As exciting as a UTI. He earns a lot, which would have made my mother happy.' She shook her head. 'He just wasn't for me.'

'Your mother was displeased?'

The meal finished, Nicola wiped her lips and her hands with the wet wipes. 'I'll tell you my mother's greatest fear. It is that I will end up married to another cop. I don't think she'd be able to live with that.' She set a gimlet eye on Rayyan. 'So watch out, Buster, in case I decide that you're the one I'm going to piss my mother off with.' She smiled. 'Honestly, Sarge, you have to do something about that blushing.'

* * *

Nicola was not the only one who had someone thinking about her. Jamie Pearson would never have asked Theresa McErlane to become Theresa Pearson, and Theresa had known that, and so she had asked him. Except that she hadn't, because instead of asking him, she had told him. Both of them knew that, and both were glad that Theresa had made the effort. Jamie had no wish to be anything other than a uniformed constable driving a police car and looking for ways to make other people safer. Theresa, even as a young uniformed constable learning on the job with Jamie as a teacher, had set her heart on a career as a detective. She had moved into the Major Crimes Investigation Team after using her brain in combination with the sheer nosiness without which no detective can hope to succeed. She had, at the same time, kept Jamie from becoming the latest victim of two female serial killers. And she was well aware that it was a growing love for the street smart but so innocent Jamie that had driven her. When he seemed not to understand why her nightie was under a pillow on his bed and her clothes in his drawers, she had explained that it was because they were going to marry.

Theresa was pretty confident after almost a year of marriage that Jamie was grateful to her. What she didn't know was just how grateful. It still seemed astonishing to Jamie that Theresa was prepared to take off her clothes and climb into bed with him. He loved her. And at times like this, when the MCIT was up to its ears in work and he saw Theresa only briefly as she showered, ate, slept, showered again, dressed and left for work, he worried about her.

Which was why, when she was leaving the house that morning, Jamie handed her a bag. 'In case you forget to eat.' Inside was a bottle of water, a hard-boiled egg, two cold grilled sausages, a tomato, two slices of wholemeal bread, buttered and with the buttered sides facing each other, and a little paper wrap of salt.

Just for a moment, tears came to Theresa's eyes. Even today, a police force was still a masculine if not a macho environment. The values most people were ready to express were masculine values. But Theresa knew what she was looking at inside this bag. She was looking at totally committed love. When it was time, she carried her lunch to a desk in the incident room and ate it with feelings of great happiness.

* * *

The conversation in that incident room was about very little other than the murders they were dealing with. Another conversation about the same subject was going on between two men in a London club.

'Our orders were for one killing. Now three men are dead. What does that tell us?'

'That the killer is not under our total control.'

'And he is...? Who?'

'The name he goes under is Thomas Westwood. But everyone calls him Westwood.'

'Tell me about him.'

'I'd prefer not to do that. He has a big name in that part of the world. For which we are responsible. We built a legend for him and spread it among certain people. People who don't like the law, or think it doesn't apply to them. They believe Westwood has killed five people. And so he has, but not the five that people in Batterton think he's killed. Under a different name, he spent ten years in Special Forces. There was no difficulty finding people to kill then, and the government paid him for it.'

'I don't understand. Why did we want to frighten people there?'

'We didn't. He did a job for us in... Well, you don't need to know where it was. And it didn't go as well as it might have done. Probably because Westwood has been quietly going off his rocker, but we didn't keep close enough tabs so we didn't know that. We sent him up to Batterton to lie low and stay out of trouble. His contact there was Harold Frobisher. Frobisher was supposed to look after him. Make sure he had enough to occupy him. Provide the occasional woman. Keep him fed and watered. But Frobisher already has too many irons in the fire and he clearly didn't spend enough time with Westwood to know his grasp on reality was getting even more stretched. What we know now is that Westwood has been visiting some of the low-life areas. Like the one where Cedric Bartholomew lived. He's been burnishing his image. Scaring the shit out of people. But we didn't know that before, because Frobisher dropped the ball. Then Frobisher passed on Jensen Bartholomew's request for help, there was some urgency about it, no one else was immediately available and Westwood was there. So we decided to use him, just that once.'

'We? Cantrell, you sometimes use that word a little loosely.'

'All right, I. I decided. And at first I thought it had gone well. Cedric Bartholomew was his legitimate target. We contracted him for that and we paid him. He was supposed to put public frighteners on his brother. Very public, because that was the whole point. He was not supposed to kill anyone else. And as far as we can tell, the nightwatchman was an accident. He was hit too hard. Shit happens. But the other guy…'

'Ali Badaan?'

'Him. It's very clear Westwood chose to kill him. It was a conscious decision.'

'Westwood. How much does he know?'

'If you mean, can he point the finger at us or Jensen Bartholomew, I think the answer is no. There's not one but two cut-outs between us and Westwood. He and I have never met, not even when he was Special Forces. We recruited him through the Iranian embassy.'

'Are you joking?'

'Where else would someone like Westwood go if he wanted employment? The only country that executes more people than Iran is China. People make a terrible fuss when Saudi Arabia buys a British football club, but the Saudis don't kill anything like the number Iran do. Iran's average is three a day. They killed three yesterday, they're killing three today, they'll kill three tomorrow. Most of them are hanged in public from very high cranes. The idea is to make sure the population remains cowed into submission. But occasionally they want someone executed in someone else's country. Westwood was just the man. He pulled one here in London; we caught him and offered him a deal. Work for us or spend the rest of your life in a high security jail.

'Should we be worried?'

'I think so. Westwood knows he was told to kill Cedric, and he knows he was told to threaten the other Bartholomew, but not to go anywhere near him. Who those orders came from he has no idea. Killing Badaan was not in his remit. And nor was leaving a message on Badaan's body telling Jensen Bartholomew he'd be next. That was all down to Westwood. He seems to have thought he was acting in a pantomime. Or maybe he's just bored.'

'Do you think he'll go after Bartholomew? Turn his threats into action?'

'If he does, the whole operation will have been for nothing. This was supposed to be a clean-up, not a bloodbath.'

'What about Frobisher's wife? The MP?'

'You just said it. She's an MP. She only knows what it's in her interest to know, and if it stops being in her interest she'll forget it immediately. We don't need to worry about her.'

'Are we safe if we leave Westwood roaming around?'

'No, we aren't. I'm sending someone from here to take care of it. Someone reliable. And someone whose balls we have in a vice, so if anything goes wrong he won't point anyone in our direction.'

'I think I'd prefer not to know what we have on this mystery killer.'

'Very wise. And I'll tell Frobisher that it's all being taken care of.'

'Those files. Did we ever find out what's in them?'

'We have no idea.'

As it happens, that last sentence was not true. Cantrell knew exactly what was in the files, because he had them safely locked up. It wasn't information he found necessary to share. His plan was not to use what was in the files, but to prevent anyone else from doing so.

* * *

The next briefing took place several hours later. There was a sense of fatigue, but also a feeling that the right things were being done and sooner or later they'd know the name of their killer.

Blazeley said, 'Let's go through what you've all been doing. The sooner we get it done, the sooner we can all go home for some sleep. But don't rush anything. We don't know yet what is going to turn out to be important. Who's first?'

Sally Christmas said, 'The DNA on the sock that was filled with weights and used as a club to batter Yuri Malinov to death. It belongs to someone called Del Theobald.'

'Well done, Sally. Do we know this guy?'

Keys were being tapped furiously at keyboards all over the room, and then a detective sergeant said, 'Major Crimes don't, but uniform certainly do. He's a thug. Eighteen convictions, for grievous bodily harm and actual bodily harm – and a Not Guilty for attempted murder. Defence counsel has usually been able to get him off with a suspended sentence, but he has served a total of seven years. He's on probation right now after his last release, so it shouldn't be too difficult to find out where he lives.'

'Get an arrest team together and nick him for murder,' said Blazeley. 'Tell them to arrest him for the murder of Yuri Malinov, caution him, and bring him back to the cells. Make sure he has a lawyer, whether he wants one or not. And tell them to be careful.'

'I don't think they'll need that,' said Theresa. 'They know just what a nutter he is. I remember the last time we had to pick him up. It took me and three men to get him cuffed and put him in a car.'

'Okay,' said Blazeley. 'Anything else?'

'Sir,' said Nicola. 'Is it just me? Or is there something odd about this whole thing?'

'Say some more about that?'

'You've got two brothers. One of them lives in a broken-down dump, he doesn't have any money, breaking into his house would be a piece of cake, and none of the neighbours would take any notice if you killed him. The other lives in a house with the latest thing in alarms and he's so loaded that as soon as he thinks his life might be in danger he hires 24-hour protection. You want to kill them both. Which one are you going to do first?'

A low murmur of conversation went round the room. Blazeley said, 'I see what you mean. Kill Jensen Bartholomew first, Cedric Bartholomew will still be there. You can go after him at your leisure. But kill Cedric first and killing Jensen becomes a great deal harder.'

'And let's not forget, boss,' said Nicola, 'that Jensen Bartholomew received two warnings. Two. To make sure he was really on his guard.'

'So what's your theory, Nicola?'

'Suppose whoever is behind all this doesn't want to kill Jensen Bartholomew. What they want is to make him so scared that he hands over... Well, I don't know what they want him to hand over. But they would assume that he does know.'

Blazeley said, 'I think that theory stands up. From here on, we run with two possible theories about why Cedric Bartholomew was killed. One says that the threat to his brother is serious; the other says it isn't, but that his brother has something the killer wants. We keep both of those ideas side-by-side until one of them is disproved.'

* * *

As requested by Blazeley, four uniformed officers were sent to find Del Theobald and arrest him. Although he was on duty, Jamie Pearson wasn't one of the four, because the control room had sent him and his new mentee, Constable Ashley Yeo, to investigate a phone call that said someone had reported a body in St Marys churchyard. 'Probably a drunk,' said Jamie. 'They congregate in that churchyard. And probably not dead. Just sleeping it off. We'll give him a nice comfortable cell to do that in.'

But when they reached the churchyard, they found it wasn't a drunk and he really was dead. Shot twice in the chest and then again in the forehead. A professional killing. 'Do you know him?' asked Constable Yeo.

Jamie shook his head. 'I don't think I've ever seen him. Call it in, will you? We need to get Scenes of Crime out here.'

* * *

Del Theobald had fought the four officers sent to arrest him every inch of the way. When they dragged him through the door into the custody suite, it would have been difficult to say who looked the worse for wear – him or them. The custody sergeant sighed. She'd had to deal with Theobald before. 'Why have you brought this man here?'

'Mr Theobald has been arrested on suspicion of murder.'

'What are the circumstances?'

'A guard was beaten to death outside an office building. Mr Theobald has been forensically linked to the murder. The major crimes investigation team asked us to carry out the arrest.'

The custody sergeant said to Theobald, 'Do you understand why you've been arrested? You have been brought here for questioning in regard to a murder investigation. I'm going to authorise your detention to secure and preserve evidence and obtain evidence by questioning. Do you understand? Take the handcuffs off him and search him, please.' To Theobald, she said, 'Would you like a copy of the code of practice that tells you what you should expect and what you are entitled to while you are in custody?'

'Has it changed since I was last here?'

The sergeant checked the record. 'Three months ago? No, I don't think it's changed in that time.'

'Then I don't want to see it. I do want a lawyer.'

That exchange had been tongue in cheek on the custody sergeant's side, because she knew from previous experience that Del Theobald was unable to read. She wasn't prepared to make fun of him on that account, though she knew some of the officers did, and in any case the custody regulations were clear. She had to offer the code of practice, and so she did. She also offered him an appropriate adult but, as ever, he refused. 'The duty solicitor today is Mr Bonser. You know the routine. I'll put you in a cell and he'll see you as soon as he's available. I'm also going to get a doctor to take a look at you.'

'I should think so.' He pointed at the officers who'd brought him in. 'I was ready to come peacefully, but your hooligans beat me up for fun.'

'Is that so, Mr Theobald? I think we'd better get the doctor to look at them, too. Just in case you get ideas about claiming compensation.'

Theobald was photographed standing against a chart that indicated his height. Then his fingerprints and DNA swabs were taken, although both were already on file, and he was escorted to a cell.

CHAPTER 9

There were times when Cyril Bonser wondered why the criminal law, and particularly working as a defence lawyer, had ever appealed to him. It was almost two hours after Del Theobald had been put in a cell before Bonser made his way there. He had defended Theobald before, more than once, and at no time had he ever thought he was innocent. He doubted it now – but defending Theobald was his job and he would do it. His aim would be what it had always been: to mitigate the damage. To get a murder charge downgraded to manslaughter and to get the sentence as low as possible. Ideally, to get it suspended – though that wasn't going to happen on a charge as serious as this. But two murder charges? Because the police had disclosed as little as they could get away with, which was what they always did and what he would have done in their place, but they had had to mention Ali Badaan. This was going to be yet one more uphill struggle. Others before him had transferred to the Crown Prosecution Service where, instead of defending the indefensible, they had helped the police prosecute the guilty. Perhaps the time was near when Bonser needed to consider that move.

While Theobald waited for Cyril Bonser he was given a mug of tea. He also received a visit from a doctor who confirmed that he was fit to be interviewed. Eventually, he was taken from his cell to an interview room where Bonser greeted him like the old customer he was. Bonser said, 'A man called Yuri Malinov was clubbed outside the office building where he worked as a night-time security guard. He died. The police have the weapon and it has your DNA on it. Did you kill Malinov?'

Both men had enough experience to know the significance of this moment. What they had to work on was Theobald's future – and where he would spend it. The aim was that the least possible part of it should be in prison. If the police had the weapon and the weapon had Theobald's DNA on it, then in the absence of a serious technical error by the police – and technical errors by the police were not uncommon – there was no chance of a Not Guilty verdict. That was the basis they had to work on. Theobald said, 'I didn't mean to. Maybe I hit him too hard. And maybe he had a thin skull – you'll need to check that.'

'Were you breaking into the office building?'

Theobald shook his head. 'That was someone else's job. Mine was just to make sure there was no guard around when it happened.'

'Do you know who it was?'

'You're not asking me to grass, Mr Bonser?'

'It's entirely your choice, Del. All I can do is advise you. And my advice right now is that we offer a deal. You admit you hit him, you didn't intend to kill him, we go for manslaughter and not murder – but if you want to deal, you need something to offer. If you don't want to tell me who followed you in there, you don't have to. But you are depriving yourself of something that might shorten your sentence.' He waited. People like Theobald might talk disparagingly about grasses, but they were usually good evidence that there was no honour among thieves.

'What do you think you can get me, Mr Bonser?'

'You mean, your sentence? That's a question for defence counsel, and we won't be appointing them for a long time yet. It's also, as you well know, something of a lottery – it depends on what judge we get and there's no way to control that.'

'Okay. I don't know all the ins and outs, because this job didn't come in the usual way.'

'It wasn't Winkleman?'

Theobald shook his head. 'Some woman I never saw before. Said she was up from London and needed a guard taken out. She said someone was going to break into the building, and the guard had to be got out of the way before the someone arrived. My job was just the guard, and then I was to leave. I got a hundred quid for it.'

'So you don't actually know who followed you?'

Theobald sat for a moment in silence and then said, 'I didn't exactly say that, Mr Bonser.'

'I see. You hung around after you'd dealt with the guard.'

'I was curious. Usually, if someone hires you for a job, you know what's happening. It's Winkleman, or someone else but someone local, but usually it's Winkleman. And Winkleman likes to tell you the score. Especially if it's someone like it was that night. Someone whose name would scare you.'

'You've got my attention, Del, you must know that.'

'Yes. Anyway. I hit the guard – I just meant to knock him out, not to kill him – and I dragged him into the trees. I was supposed to leave then. I'd been paid my hundred quid upfront.'

'But you didn't.'

'As I say, I was curious. So I stayed in the trees with the guard. He was still making funny little noises, so I didn't think… I didn't mean to kill him, Mr Bonser.'

'You said that, Del. So who showed up?'

'Ali Badaan.'

'Ali Badaan? That's hardly a name that would scare you.'

'No. And he was real spiffy – there wasn't much light, but with what there was I could see he wasn't wearing the kind of clothes you put on for a job like that. In fact, he wasn't wearing what he usually wore at all.'

'And he wasn't the last, was he? Because his job would have been to deal with the alarms. Not to break in.'

'That's right, Mr Bonser. And that's what he did. At least, I didn't see him do it, but that's what Ali Badaan does.'

'Did, Del.'

'What?'

'Don't you read the papers? Ali Badaan is as dead as the guard, Del.'

'I can't read, Mr Bonser. I thought you knew that. But Ali – dead?'

'Stone cold, Del. Throat cut from ear to ear. And you know what the police are going to think. In fact, they've already told me they want you on both charges.'

Theobald had turned white. 'What? They're not going to try to stick that on me?'

'Why wouldn't they? You were there. And you'd already killed one man. You know the way the police think. Clear up two cases in one.'

'Mr Bonser. I didn't! The guard, yes, but Ali Badaan – no!'

'I believe you, Del. But it isn't about what I believe. And, in any case, you'd better hope the two killings are totally separate incidents. Otherwise, you could be convicted of the Badaan murder under the Joint Enterprise principle. So tell me what happened next.'

'I stayed in the trees. Ali Badaan was inside the building. I suppose he was waiting to be paid, although that wasn't the way it was usually done. Then someone came out of the trees only about ten feet from me. I watched him walk across the car park. And I left. I wanted nothing to do with anything he was in.'

'He being…?'

'Westwood, Mr Bonser. It was Westwood. But we can't tell the police that.'

'Westwood?'

'You're not going to say you don't know who I'm talking about?'

'It's a name I've heard, Del.' From time to time, he thought, and in hushed tones. 'But I've never met him and I've never heard that he was ever involved in any case.'

'He's killed five people that I know of, Mr Bonser. Say Westwood to some of the hardest men in this town, they'll turn to jelly. But, no, he's never been in court and I don't think he's even been arrested.'

'And you don't want the police to know he was there?'

'Mr Bonser. If they did stick Ali's murder on me, what's the worst I could get? I'd still be out sometime – right?

Even if I need a wheelchair to get around, I'll still have time for a few afternoons in the pub, a few knee tremblers, the odd fiver on a horse before they measure me for the wooden box. But if I get on the wrong side of Westwood, I don't have any of that to look forward to. Westwood would off me and he'd enjoy doing it. No. You can't tell the police.'

'All right, Del. On your head be it. I'm going to write your statement. Then I'll read it to you so you know what you're saying. We'll tell the police we are ready, I'll read the statement to them and I'll say you're not answering any questions. You know what you have to do then, right?'

'Keep my trap shut?'

'Exactly. And they'll try to get you to say something. But you don't do it. You know the score, Del. Once upon a time, when it would have been my father sitting here and your father where you are, the police might have tried to beat a confession out of you. That's why we have PACE. They can't do that now, because every interview has to be videoed. So now they have specialist trained interviewers who don't do anything else. In this station they have Gareth Forester and Sally Barnes and you won't find anybody better at the job than them. There are no tricks they don't know, and they will do everything they can to get you to say something you shouldn't. The only way to avoid that is to say nothing. Now just keep quiet for a while and I'll write this statement.'

* * *

As Cyril Bonser had expected, the interview was run by detective constables Gareth Forester and Sally Barnes. Whatever Del Theobald might have seen on television, no one was watching through a one-way mirror, because there aren't any of those in the UK. The interview *was* watched, though, because DCI Bill Blazeley and DI Susanna David were following it on monitors in another room. New information gleaned from CCTV cameras on the business estate had arrived a few minutes earlier, and they had passed it on to Gareth and Sally while briefing them on the background to the interview. In theory, this information should also have been given to Cyril Bonser as the defence lawyer, but the police always interpreted that rule loosely and always in their favour. They had told Bonser that they had his client's DNA on the murder weapon. What more could he expect?

Gareth started the tape and each of the four people in the room identified themselves in their own voices to make it easier for a transcriber to identify who was speaking by the sound of their voice without having to run the video at the same time. Then Cyril Bonser said, 'My client wishes to place on file a prepared statement, which I will now read to you. My client will not answer any questions after that.'

This brought a quiet smile from both interviewers, and Sally said, 'Go ahead and read the statement. We reserve the right to question your client afterwards.'

'You can reserve any rights you like,' said Bonser. 'And you can ask any questions you like. But you won't get any answers. Here is the statement.' And then he proceeded to read the statement as though he had been Del Theobald himself. 'I was offered a sum of money to incapacitate the night watchman at the Bartholomew Group office building. The woman who made this offer was not known to me. She was not local and she said she had come up from London. I accepted the assignment. I was paid one hundred pounds for it and I received the money in advance. On the night I had been told to do so, I hid near the building until the night watchman was making his rounds. I stepped up behind him and hit him over the head with a sock into which I had inserted weights. It was not my intention to kill him and I believe that a medical examination may establish that he had a particularly thin skull. I moved the body into the trees as gently as possible. Then I left. When I left, Yuri Malinov was still alive and I repeat that I did not believe I had hit him hard enough to kill him. My suspicion is that he was actually killed by someone who came after me. I had nothing to do with any subsequent killing'

Bonser passed the written statement across the table. 'Mr Theobald has made his mark and I have witnessed it. He will answer no questions. In view of his helpfulness in furnishing this statement, I request that he now be released on bail.'

Gareth actually laughed at that last sentence and Sally said, 'Well, bail might be a little difficult to arrange, this being a murder case. And the statement you have so helpfully read out deals with only one killing. Mr Theobald is here because we suspect him of two murders. Mr Theobald, three of the office buildings along the road the Bartholomew building is on have CCTV cameras that cover anyone moving up and down the road.' She paused, hoping to see a sign of concern on Theobald's face. She was not disappointed. She went on, 'We are now going to show you a recording taken the night Yuri Malinov and Ali Badaan died.'

Onto the screen came Theobald, walking down the road in the direction of the Bartholomew Group building. The time stamp said it was 9:45. Theobald entered the Bartholomew car park and they lost sight of him. Someone the police assumed to be Ali Badaan had deleted the Bartholomew Group CCTV recording, but they saw no need to tell Theobald or his lawyer that. Sally said, 'Is that you, Mr

Theobald?' Theobald looked at Bonser, who shook his head. With an effort obvious to everyone in the room, Theobald remained silent. Sally said, 'For the recording, Mr Theobald has declined to answer the question. What does it show you doing?' After another pause, she said, 'Mr Theobald has once again declined to answer the question. Do you agree, Mr Theobald, that you are trying not to be seen?' Another glance from prisoner to lawyer, another shake of the head and then, 'Mr Theobald has once more declined to answer the question.'

At 10.20, Ali Badaan passed down the same road and entered the Bartholomew car park. Sally said. 'Who is that entering the Bartholomew car park, Mr Theobald?' The silences were having no effect on Sally and Gareth but Blazely and Susanna watching on their monitors would have known they were looking at a man on the verge of breaking. Sally said, 'That was Ali Badaan, wasn't it? He arrived and you were still in the car park. Why did you say you hadn't seen anyone else after you clubbed Yuri Malinov?' No response. Then, at 10.40, the screen showed Theobald leaving the car park. Gareth said, 'Is that you, Del, leaving the car park twenty minutes after Ali Badaan entered it?' No reply. 'What were you doing in the twenty minutes that elapsed between Ali Badaan's arrival at the Bartholomew building and your departure?'

No one could have missed the fear on Theobald's face as he listened to what the interviewers were telling him. He turned to Cyril Bonser and Bonser gave the very slightest shake of his head. Theobald turned back to the two interviewers and looked at them in silence. When it became clear he was not going to answer the question, Gareth said, 'Isn't that when you killed Ali Badaan, Del?'

Everything about Theobald's face and posture said that he was terrified, but he said nothing.

Sally said, 'It's the only explanation. Isn't it? You were in the Bartholomew building car park when Ali Badaan went in there. You stayed for twenty minutes, which means you were there at the time that Ali Badaan was killed. And you've already admitted to killing Yuri Malinov.' Theobald moved forward in his chair as if about to speak, but Cyril Bonser put a hand on his arm and Theobald remained silent. Sally went on, 'As for the suggestion that someone else might have finished off your first victim for you, we've checked CCTV right through to the time people start arriving for work. No one else is visible. So, Del, unless you can offer an alternative explanation, we are now going to ask the opinion of our senior officers. I expect them to ask the CPS to instruct us to charge you with the murders of Yuri Malinov and Ali Badaan. Have you anything to say?'

After a quick glance in Cyril Bonser's direction,

Theobald remained silent. Gareth and Sally stood up. 'Very well,' said Sally. 'If we can't save you from your own foolishness, we can't. We'll leave you for a few minutes to discuss your predicament with your lawyer.'

'Two murder charges, Del,' said Gareth. 'If you're convicted, that's two mandatory life sentences. Talk to Mr Bonser while we are away and see if you can come up with a more sensible approach.'

When they were gone, Cyril Bonser said to Theobald, 'You are sure about... About the third man? I won't mention his name – I know they've turned off the recorder, but I'm never 100% certain you can trust the police when they say they're not listening in. But he doesn't seem to have been picked up by the same CCTV that saw you and Ali Badaan.'

'He didn't come down the road, Mr Bonser. He came through the other trees. Not the ones overlooking the road, the ones at the back of the car park. He knew what he was doing – I should have had enough sense to do the same. What's going to happen now?'

'You know what's going to happen. You've been here before. Not for murder, but you know the routine. Those two will come back, you'll be held in the cells overnight and tomorrow they'll put you in front of a magistrate and get you remanded. There's no point asking for bail because, in a murder case, magistrates have no power to grant it.'

'I wouldn't ask for it if they had,' said Theobald. 'I don't want to be out while you know who is running around. It would be just like him to see me as a loose end that he needs to tidy up. Like he tidied up Ali Badaan.'

Bonser was partly right in what he had described. Gareth Forester and Sally Barnes, having spoken to Bill Blazeley and Susanna David, did come back and tell Del Theobald that he would be charged with the murders of Ali Badaan and Yuri Malinov. Theobald was locked up in a cell overnight and told he'd be put before a magistrate in the morning with the request that his case be referred to the Crown Court. But something happened that meant there was a little hiatus before that trip to the magistrate's court came about.

The SOCOs who had attended the body discovered by PCs Jamie Pearson and Ashley Yeo had found a wallet in the dead man's pocket. It contained a debit card and credit cards. The cards bore a man's name. They hadn't got much further than that but, in the usual way, a press release had been issued saying that a body had been found in Saint Mary's churchyard, the police regarded the death as suspicious, and the body had been identified as Thomas Westwood. The editor of *The Post* had given the release to reporter Bernadette Spence and Bernadette had written up the story. She hadn't been able to put any flesh on the bones, because Thomas Westwood was not mentioned anywhere in *The Post*'s voluminous archives. As far as Bernie could tell, he'd never been in any kind of trouble.

* * *

When Cyril Bonser arrived for work the next morning, he picked up the copy of *The Post* his secretary had left on his desk. It took a while to reach the story about the late Thomas Westwood because it was on an inside page as befitted its lack of importance in the mind of the *Post*'s editor, but the moment Bonser saw it he turned to the keyboard on his desk and began to write a new statement for Del Theobald to make his mark on. Then he set off for the police station.

When he got there, he got the custody sergeant's confirmation that Del Theobald had not yet been taken to court. 'The prison van broke down on the way here,' said the sergeant. 'That's what happens when you subcontract these things to private enterprise. It might be the afternoon before we get him out of here. Do you want to see him?'

'Yes, please. And if the senior investigating officer on the Ali Badaan case is available, I'd like to see him right afterwards. Please,' he added when the custody sergeant glared at him.

Del Theobald seemed to be having trouble taking in what Cyril Bonser was telling him. 'Westwood? Dead? Are they sure?'

'It's in the paper, Del.'

'How did he die?'

'We don't know that yet. But he's dead. So I've expanded your statement a little. Let me tell you what it says.'

* * *

A little later, Bonser and Theobald were back in the interview room with Gareth Forester and Sally Barnes. If Bonser was disappointed that Bill Blazeley was not there, he didn't let it show. He was, in any case, very sure that Blazeley and Susanna David would have briefed the two interviewers thoroughly and would be watching on a monitor somewhere in the building. He was not wrong.

Gareth started the recording equipment and all four people present gave their names. 'Mr Theobald,' said Sally. 'What you have asked for is unusual. I want you to understand why we have agreed to it and what can and cannot happen at this interview. You were charged yesterday with the murders of Yuri Malinov and Ali Badaan. The Police and Criminal Evidence Act says that, once you have been charged with an offence, you can only be questioned further in relation to that offence if the questions are absolutely necessary for one of three purposes. That requirement is not for our benefit, Mr Theobald – it's for yours. It's there to protect you. One of the three purposes is to provide you with an opportunity to comment on information concerning the offence you have been charged with which has come to light since you were charged and if it is in the interests of justice to do so. Do you understand that?'

Theobald nodded.

'Mr Theobald has nodded in what we take to be confirmation that he understands what he has just been told. And this new information is the only thing we can discuss at this interview. Please don't try to introduce anything else. Is that clear?'

'Yes. Yes, it is.'

'Very well. You were cautioned before the last interview began. I will caution you again now. You are under arrest on suspicion of murder. You do not have to say anything, but it may harm your defence if you do not mention when questioned something which you later rely on in court. Anything you do say may be given in evidence. You've changed your statement, Mr Theobald. Why?'

Theobald looked at Bonser and Bonser nodded. He had given his client very detailed instructions on what he could say and what he could not. Theobald said, 'I was terrified, Mrs Barnes.'

The ghost of a smile passed across Sally's face. 'It's Ms Barnes, Del. Though "Officer" will do nicely. What were you terrified of?'

'Not what, Ms… Officer. Who. Westwood, that's who.'

'Really. In your new statement, you say that Ali Badaan was still alive when you left the scene, and that you left because this man Westwood had arrived. Is that right?'

'Yes. Westwood would scare the life out of anyone.'

'Then isn't it curious that we've never heard of him here?'

Theobald looked at Bonser, and Bonser said, 'Ms Barnes, you can't expect my client to take responsibility for the shortcomings of Batterton Police. My client is liable to lose control of his bowels at the very mention of Westwood's name. And he is far from the only one in this town's criminal fraternity of whom that is true.'

Sally grinned and looked sideways at Gareth who said, 'If your story is to be believed – your new story, that is, because this is not the song you were singing yesterday – Ali Badaan was still alive and you believe that the man we'd never heard of until yesterday and now know as Thomas Westwood must have killed him. You also believe that it was Thomas Westwood who killed Yuri Malinov, even though you have already admitted having hit Malinov on the back of the head with a very heavy weapon.'

'I didn't kill anyone, Mr Foster. I've never killed anyone. Look at my record and you'll see.'

'Well, Del, let me tell you what we're going to do for you. We're going to hand over this interview to two detectives who will ask for all the information you can give them about this man, Thomas Westwood. If they are satisfied with your openness and honesty,' and at these words Gareth could not prevent himself from smiling broadly, however hard he tried, 'you will be returned to your cell. At the end of that conversation, the information you have provided will be presented to the CPS who will decide what charges should be brought against you.' And then, as though it had been prepared in advance (which it had), the door opened, DI Susanna David and DS Rayyan Padgett entered, and Gareth and Sally left. The two newcomers spoke their names for the recording.

Susanna said, 'Mr Theobald. The personnel on this side of the desk have changed, but this is still a formal interview, you are still being recorded, you are still under caution and I advise you, when you answer our questions, to confine yourself to the truth. You have told our colleagues that you went to the Bartholomew building with instructions to incapacitate the nightwatchman, Yuri Malinov. Is that correct?'

Theobald nodded. 'Yes. Yes, it is.'

'And who gave you those instructions?'

'I don't know.'

'Come on now,' said Susanna. "I thought you wanted to be honest with us? Refusing to give us information is not being honest.'

'I'd tell you if I knew. I don't. It was someone I'd never dealt with before.'

Rayyan said, 'It was Terry Winkleman. Wasn't it?'

Theobald turned shocked eyes on the Sergeant. 'Mr Padgett, you know better than that.'

Cyril Bonser intervened. 'Sergeant Padgett, If you believe a man called Winkleman is involved you should disclose that to me.'

Rayyan and Susanna smiled at each other. Terry Winkleman had never been charged with anything. He covered his tracks with remarkable efficiency. But the suggestion that Cyril Bonser, one of the city's most experienced criminal lawyers, had never heard of him was enough to make any policeman smile. And so was Theobald's obvious outrage that Rayyan should have expected him to grass Winkleman up. Susanna said, 'We'll leave that, at least for now. If you didn't know who was instructing you, Mr Theobald, why would you obey the instructions?'

'Because I'd been paid. I woke up one morning and found someone had shoved an envelope through my letterbox. In the envelope were ten ten pound notes. There was no note, but that morning I got a phone call.'

'Do you still have the envelope?'

'No – I burned it.'

'Of course you did. So, the phone call… Who made it and what did it say?'

'I've no idea who made it. I didn't recognise the voice. It told me that the hundred quid was payment for taking the nightwatchman out of circulation. She gave me the place, she gave me the date, she gave me the time and she told me I'd regret it if I pocketed the money and didn't do the job.'

Susanna and Rayyan were both leaning forward. Susanna said, 'She? The caller was a woman?'

'That's right.'

'And you have no idea who it was?'

Rayyan said, 'Could it have been Terry Winkleman's wife?'

'No,' said Theobald. 'She talks like a local. This woman was posh. I mean, Princess Anne kind of posh.'

Cyril Bonser put his hand on Theobald's arm and Rayyan said, 'So you have no idea who Terry Winkleman might be, but you know what his wife sounds like,' and Bonser said, 'If you can't behave like honest people, we'll end this interview right now.'

Susanna left a break in the conversation long enough for everyone to enjoy the thought of a crook's mouthpiece demanding the police behave honestly. As she was about to speak again, Cyril Bonser said, 'Can we stick to the matter under discussion? My client has already admitted that he was hired to incapacitate the nightwatchman. He has also admitted to having hit the nightwatchman on the head, though he strenuously denies any intention to kill him. Is there any need to rehash all of that?'

Susanna said, 'Mr Bonser, you are quite right. And if your client is not prepared to name the party who instructed him…'

'It isn't that he isn't prepared, it's that he doesn't know.'

'Yes, well, so he says, and we'll leave that for now. Mr Theobald, you say that after you hit Mr Malinov and moved him into the trees where he could not be seen, you stayed on the scene.'

Theobald nodded.

'And you say you saw Ali Badaan arrive and you assumed that he was there to have the same effect on the alarm system as you had had on the nightwatchman. Is that correct?'

Theobald nodded again. 'Yes. It is.'

'Very well. Mr Badaan, as you will know, was murdered that night and in that place. And you are under suspicion for that crime, since you are the only person we know for certain to have been there.' Seeing Theobald's outraged expression and knowing that he was about to speak again, she raised a hand and said, 'But you claim to have seen the arrival of someone you name as Thomas Westwood. Is *that* correct?'

'Yes. It is.'

'Tell me everything you can about this man Thomas Westwood.'

* * *

As this conversation was coming to an end, Bernadette Spence at *The Post* was taking a phone call from a woman with an accent that spoke of money and privilege. 'Westwood. Is he really dead?'

'The police say so.'

'And your report says it was suspicious. I bet it was. Somebody caught up with him. I suppose it was always going to happen, but he always seemed such a force of nature.'

'Do you have any information for me?'

'That's what I'm calling about. What's it worth?'

'I'd have to speak to my editor, and he won't decide until we know the quality of what you have to tell us. If it's worth it, I could probably get you a hundred quid. But it has to be exclusive.'

'A hundred buys you nothing, darling.'

'How much do you want?'

'Five hundred. Minimum. It will be worth it, I promise you.'

People had made promises like that to Bernadette before. The public had inflated ideas about what newspapers were able to pay. For five hundred pounds, *The Post*'s editor expected something startlingly good. She said, 'I can't make any commitment until I know what you've got. Where can we meet?'

'You know the Parkway railway station? I'll see you outside.'

'I can be there in forty minutes. How will I recognise you?'

'You won't need to. I'll know you. Come to a halt right outside and I'll step into your car.' The line went dead.

CHAPTER 10

Forty minutes after she'd hung up on that call, Bernadette Spence pulled up outside the terminal building at the Parkway station and a woman opened the passenger side door, slid into the seat, closed the door and said, 'Drive. I'll tell you where to go.' The reporter had slipped a small digital recorder into the pocket in the door beside her, and now she switched it on. Recording someone without their permission or knowledge was not against the law, but it became illegal if the information was shared with others which was, of course, exactly what Bernie intended to do. She wasn't going to let that trouble her. The editor's warning about the law she had already broken had been like water off a duck's back.

As they left the station, Bernadette said, 'Is Becky Smith your real name?'

'It's the name I'm using with you.'

'Okay – I'm cool with that. What have you got to tell me?'

'Have you talked to your editor about money?'

'He's prepared to meet your demand if he thinks what you give me is good enough. If not, not.'

'Cash. Not a cheque.'

'Cash in your hand, Becky. And not a word to the taxman. But it has to be worth it. So tell me what it is.'

For a while, the only thing that interrupted the silence was when the woman gave Bernie instructions. "Next left." "Turn right at the phone box." "Straight on for about half a mile." Then she said, 'My name isn't Becky Smith.'

'No? Listen, Becky, you can be anyone you like with me.'

'I didn't mean I'm going to tell you who I really am. I just wanted you to understand… Well. What does it matter? I'm not the story. Westwood is.' She glanced at Bernie and then turned back to the road. 'We're nearly there. There's a layby on the left; pull in and park and I'll tell you the rest of this bit of the story. Westwood was my bit of rough.'

'Yes? How did you meet?'

'Look, I'm the one telling the story. I'll tell it my way. Okay? And there are some things you don't need to know. This bit of the story is confidential. You don't print it – it's just for background. Understood?'

Bernie nodded. 'Understood.'

'I was educated expensively. Benenden, from eleven right through to the 6th form. Art History at St Andrews. Holidays in hot, sunny places with lots of servants and all my wishes catered to. If I ever have children, and even if I have the money, I won't bring them up like that. My parents had great expectations for me and my brother. I've disappointed them.'

'What about your brother?'

'I've no idea. I haven't seen him, or either of my parents, for three years. Since I teamed up with Westwood, in fact. Never mind all of that. It's Westwood I want to talk about. He is the only bit of this you can print. So. You want to know how we met. It was in a club. Not here – in Manchester. I'd gone up there with a boyfriend. The boyfriend was someone my parents would have approved of, which is another way of saying he was the hole in the centre of the doughnut. His idea of the high life was champagne and cocaine. I expect you know the type.'

Bernadette smiled. 'I'm not sure I do, Becky. But carry on.'

'Well, we can pass over most of the next bit. It doesn't show me in a very good light. But when I left that club, I left with Westwood. I didn't realise it until later, but he'd engineered my boyfriend's disappearance. Did you ever meet Westwood?'

'If I did, I wasn't aware of it.'

Bernadette was aware that her informant's reluctance to speak was fading as she became caught up in her narrative and her memories. Or that's how it seemed, at any rate. 'Oh, you'd have been aware of it. Westwood was astonishing. I mean to look at, quite apart from anything else. He always looked as though he'd come off an F Scott Fitzgerald movie set. I'd describe him as flamboyant, but that doesn't begin to describe the man. His accent suggested he came from somewhere in the north-east. Think Jimmy Nail, but with a polished exterior. You got the feeling he could take you apart and it wouldn't trouble him. He called a taxi, took me to the station and bought me a first-class ticket back to London. Told me Manchester wasn't for me, I was to stay away from the place, if I didn't he'd find out and I wouldn't like what happened next.'

'So what did you do?'

'What he told me. That was the natural response to Westwood – you did what he told you to do. And I knew that after only an hour in his presence. I went back to London. A couple of days later, the boyfriend's parents were on the phone. Where was their son? I told them I had no idea. He'd been off his face on drink and coke, I'd asked him to stop, he wouldn't, I got angry and I went home. The day after that, the police came round. The boyfriend's parents were as moneyed and entitled as mine and they knew who to speak to to get action. The police had CCTV of me arriving at Manchester Piccadilly. They showed it to

133

me. Who was that who paid the driver? And then walked me to the ticket booth and bought me a ticket? And then walked out of the station alone after I had gone through to the trains, equally alone? I said he was some guy who had taken pity on me when he saw me leave the club after rowing with my boyfriend. They wanted to know his name and I said I didn't know it. Which was true. They said they'd checked the transactions of the ticket seller he got my ticket from at the exact time he bought it, which they had from the CCTV, but the guy had paid cash so they didn't know his name any more than I did. I said, what was the big deal? The boyfriend was as flaky as a 99. He'd turn up eventually.' She fell silent for a while. Then she said, 'But he never did.'

Bernie was beginning to worry about where this was going. A journalist can't run just any story – there are some things you have to take to the police if you don't want to face charges of obstructing them, or worse. She said, not really sure she wanted to know the answer, 'Do you know what happened to him?'

'I didn't then. I found out. Maybe I'll tell you later. Maybe it's best for you if you don't know.'

'If you really expect us to pay you five hundred pounds, you need to give us something pretty solid.'

The woman turned towards Bernie, and Bernie got her first full view of a face old beyond its years and stiff with the assumption of privilege. Her hair was brown, her eyes were brown, her skin had the healthy tan that comes from regular travel to the island homes of the wealthy. She said, 'You want to know what happened to the boyfriend? I'll show you where he ended up. Start the car.' When they were moving again, she said, 'Take the next turn on the right.'

The next turn on the right turned out to be a narrow road between tall hedges. Becky Smith said, 'Go slowly. You never know who you're going to meet on this road, and nor do you know what they've been smoking, drinking and injecting.' Bernie slowed, but they met no one coming their way. After about a mile, they reached the entrance to what had once been a magnificent house but had its best days behind it. The sign on the open gate said, Jamaica House. Becky Smith said, 'Drive in here.'

The drive was lined with lime trees that had once been pleached but had for some time been allowed to grow wild. The surface was worn and the occasional pothole caused Bernie to swerve. Becky Smith said, 'There shouldn't be anyone here right now. But, if anyone does emerge, keep driving. Whatever you do, don't stop.'

When they reached the house, Becky Smith said, 'Stay on the left. Drive round the back.' Bernie did as she was told and found that the land behind the house, which looked as though it had once been ornamental gardens, was given over to farming. Becky Smith said, 'See the pigpen?'

'I see low agricultural buildings.'

'One of those is a pigpen. Keep it in your head. And keep driving.'

After another half mile, with the agricultural buildings some distance behind them, what appeared to be a kitchen garden turned back into more ornamental gardens, sadly neglected, and then they passed through another unmarked gate and onto a road similar to the one they had left earlier. Becky Smith said, 'Turn right.'

As they headed for the main road, Becky Smith said, 'Take me back to the Parkway station. You want to know what you've just seen?'

'If it wouldn't be too much trouble. And if you want a chance of payment.'

'The house you just saw belonged to Westwood. I don't know how he came by it, but it was his.'

'And the pigpen? What was the significance of that?'

'You wanted to know what happened to the boyfriend who took me to Manchester. I'm afraid I can't answer that. But what I can tell you is that, a month or so after I'd moved into that house with Westwood, he took me out to the pigpen and showed me what was left of a pair of denim jeans. And a watch.'

Unnerved by the coolness with which Becky Smith told the story, Bernie was fairly sure she knew what was coming – and she desperately did not want to hear it.

'The watch was very distinctive,' said Becky Smith. 'I can't be 100% certain that it belonged to the boyfriend, any more than I can say the jeans did. But if I were pressed, I'd put money on it.'

Bernie felt as though what she really wanted to do was stop the car and throw up. She said, 'You think Westwood had killed him and given him to the pigs to eat?'

'I certainly think he'd fed him to the pigs. Whether or not he was dead at the time, I couldn't surmise.'

'Did you escape?'

'From what? Westwood wasn't threatening me – he was just letting me know that the boyfriend was gone. Life carried on as before.'

'Becky. I need to understand this. You believed that Westwood had killed your boyfriend and let the pigs eat him. And you stayed with Westwood. Is that right?'

'Certainly. I've never met anyone who lived a life as exciting as Westwood's. You'd have stayed, too, if you had the chance.'

Bernie saw no point in answering. She'd never met anyone like the woman calling herself Becky Smith and she thought she'd prefer never to meet anyone like her again.

As they approached Parkway station, she said, 'My editor will very likely think that's worth five hundred. But I don't have it with me, so you'll have to come to the office. We'll want a receipt, and we can kill two birds with one stone. Here's my card. Call me.'

'Bernadette, I already called you to set up this meeting. I have your number. I have your home number and address, too. I'll be in touch. Rely on it.'

She was about to get out of the car when Bernie said, 'Just a moment. Westwood took you to Manchester Piccadilly station. He left you there. You took the train to London. So how did you come to be at Jamaica House for Westwood to show you the pigpen?'

'He came for me, one day in London. Told me to bring whatever I thought I didn't want to be without and to get into his car.'

'And you did?'

'I've already told you, Westwood was a man who, if he told you to do something, you did it. I went with him and I stayed with him.'

'In Jamaica House?'

'In Jamaica House. We had visitors from time to time. Criminal visitors. Or so Westwood said, and I believe him. He also told me the boyfriend wasn't the only death he'd been responsible for. This has been a taster. You've had all

£500 buys you. If you want the names of some of the visitors, and the other people Westwood killed, we'll have to negotiate. I think that's worth two grand, don't you? But if you want a slightly bigger taster, I'll give you one of the names. Cedric Bartholomew. I'll be in touch.' Bernie sat and watched her climb the stairs into the station. Full of horror as the story she had just heard had been, what stayed in her memory and turned her heart cold were the words that had been almost the last spoken to her. "I have your phone number and address."

Bernadette shivered. She went into the station, bought a packet of cigarettes and a lighter, went back to her car and began to smoke for the first time in years.

* * *

There'd been no sign in the station of Becky Smith. But, on the opposite side of the station, another car was leaving and Becky Smith was in it, being driven this time by the brother she had told Bernie she'd heard nothing from for three years. He said, 'How did it go?'

'Like a dream.'

'She bought it?'

'Hook, line and sinker. And we got a bonus.'

'Yes?'

139

'The poor cow thought I hadn't spotted her recorder. She was recording the whole conversation.'

Her brother smiled. 'Well done, Annabelle. A bonus indeed.'

CHAPTER 11

At the briefing that evening, Susanna said, 'I'll give you a precis of what Theobald told us. How much faith we can place in it, I don't know – let's not forget this is a man who wants to turn one murder charge into manslaughter and get out from under a second murder charge. But this is what he told us, shorn of all the criminal claptrap and exaggeration.

'Thomas Westwood, always known only as Westwood, is one of those Mr Big criminal characters you read about in books, see on the screen, but somehow never meet when you're going about your normal police business. This man we have never heard of is supposedly responsible for five murders. And yet, his fingerprints and DNA are not on file, because he's never been arrested. In fact, so far as I've been able to check, his name has never come up in connection with any investigation anywhere, ever. What does he live on? Nobody knows. Where does he come from? Nobody knows. Does he have a family? Wife, girlfriend, children, father, mother? Nobody knows. No one knows where he lives, either, but he is well enough known to the people of criminal enclaves in our city that they identified him when he entered a house in Dryden Close even though they couldn't see his face because he was wearing a long black cloak and a Guy Fawkes mask.' There was a stir in the room and Susanna said, 'Yes, that's right, Thomas Westwood killed Cedric Bartholomew. According to Del Theobald, at any rate. And his very presence at the Bartholomew building was enough to terrify Del Theobald, one of our more notable thugs and a man apparently ready to take on all comers, into silence. Terrified him so much that Theobald was only prepared to name Westwood when he heard that Westwood was dead – shot in Saint Mary's churchyard in what appears to have been a professional elimination. Until Theobald made his claim, we had no reason to connect that killing with the murder of Cedric Bartholomew, but I've agreed with DCI Blazeley that we should consider the crimes as connected at least until we have firm evidence that they are not.' She looked at Bill Blazeley. 'Sir, SOCO are at the churchyard right now. Charlie is the Crime Scene Manager and I imagine he'll be at tomorrow's briefing to bring us up to date. In the meantime, I suggest we treat everything I just said as an interesting insight into the mind of mentally challenged hooligans like Theobald and continue with the briefing as though we'd never heard of him.'

'I agree,' said Blazeley. 'The whole thing sounds like something out of fiction. I take it we are still holding Theobald?'

'Yes,' said Susanna. 'We know from his own admission that he was there at or about the time Ali Badaan died, but apart from that circumstantial evidence we have no forensics to tie him to that murder. He has, however, confessed to the blow to Yuri Malinov's head. Later this afternoon we'll put him in front of a magistrate and ask for him to be remanded in custody on a manslaughter charge. The Crown Prosecution Service is going to have some questions for us before that case ever gets to trial. The most important of those is going to be whether the blow Theobald struck actually killed him and Bonser will do his best to move the blame onto Thomas Westwood. Whether we'll ever get Theobald in front of a jury is not something I'd want to take a bet on. But he's under arrest and that has given us the right to search his home. I hope something will come of that – if not on this case, then on others.'

'All right,' said Blazeley. 'Thanks, Susanna, and well done. Everyone, before we move on, something I want you all doing over the next twenty-four hours is asking every contact you have whether the name Westwood means anything to them. And I'll be asking uniform to do the same thing. Now. Who's got something for us on the Cedric Bartholomew and Ali Badaan enquiries?'

A uniformed constable appeared in the doorway. 'Excuse me, sir. There's a Ms Patel in reception asking for Sergeant Padgett. She says she only has ten minutes.'

Blazeley looked towards Rayyan, who said, 'I'd better see her, Sir. She's the lawyer whose office the files were taken from. Cedric Bartholomew's fingerprint was found at the scene. Theresa Pearson and I called there and were sent away like naughty schoolchildren.'

Blazeley nodded. 'Go ahead. Theresa, you go with him. I don't think we'll be here much longer – let's hear your report on what she has to say first thing in the morning.'

CHAPTER 12

Adina Patel was tall and slim and exuded the kind of determination that the Bible said could move mountains. She also radiated contempt for the people she was speaking to. She said, 'I was told you want to see me in relation to a murder enquiry. I have no idea what information you think I possess, but I can give you ten minutes.'

Rayyan said, 'The murder in question is that of a man called Cedric Bartholomew.'

Ms Patel looked blank. 'I don't believe I know the name. What has it to do with me?'

'You reported a break-in at your office. I understand three files were taken.'

'We lost three files, that's true. Whether they were taken by whoever broke into our office, I'm not sure. Really, it seems unlikely, because the only other thing they took was a small amount of money. That made me assume it was children – and what would children want with my files?'

'It seems unlikely that children were responsible. I understand you have a fairly sophisticated alarm system and that it was bypassed. It's unlikely children could have done that. In fact, the local man most likely to have been able to turn your alarm off was also killed recently. A man called Ali Badaan – did you know him?'

Rayyan was aware that the face on the head being shaken was giving nothing away. No emotion, no knowledge, no hint of understanding. She said, 'I saw his name in *The Post*. Other than that, I've never heard of him.'

'No? Well, another reason for supposing that your burglars were not children is that a fingerprint was found. We couldn't identify it at the time, but we now know that it belonged to Cedric Bartholomew.'

'Right. I understand now why you wanted to speak to me, but I still don't know what I could possibly have to tell you.'

'Someone broke into your office to steal three files. They must have had a reason. Could you please tell me what was in those files?'

'Sergeant. I deal exclusively in asylum cases. I represent people in fear of their lives in the place they come from and the wish to be allowed to live here in peace but of whom the government would rather wash its hands. The official preference is to send them back, which often means sending them to their deaths. Every citizen of this country, Sergeant, has blood on their hands. Including me, and including you – but I at least try to do something about it.'

'I don't doubt that you do a vital and valuable job, but the files...'

'The files, like all of our files, contained information that is highly confidential because, in the wrong hands, it could lead to someone's death. We protect that confidentiality at all costs. I cannot... I will not... Tell you what was in them.' She stood up. 'Are we done?' Without waiting for a reply, she turned and left the room.

Theresa, who had not said a word throughout, stared at Rayyan. 'Can she get away with that?'

Rayyan looked tired. 'We could set about making her life difficult. But should we? She's uncooperative, she has a conceit that is almost certainly inflated... ' and then he laughed. 'But you have to admire her, don't you? For sheer self-regard, if nothing else.'

* * *

Bernadette Spence's pride was obvious as she walked into the editor's office after finishing her story and clicking SEND to put it in front of him. The look of admiration she'd hoped to see on his face was absent. He said, 'Bernie. Are you trying to get us into trouble?' Seeing her raised eyebrows, he went on, 'Joanna Yeates. Christopher Jefferies. Do those names ring a bell?'

Bernie nodded. 'We covered the story in college. But what has that to do with me?'

The editor sighed. 'Christopher Jefferies was arrested for the murder of Joanna Yeates. He shouldn't have been – there was no forensic evidence linking him to the killing at all and, in fact, he didn't do it. But the newspapers went to town on him. They said some things they shouldn't have said – in fact, they were a disgrace to the profession. The damage those newspapers did to journalism has still not been undone. They took innuendo, third party tittle tattle and downright untruths and turned them into a hatchet job on an innocent man. A retired teacher who had probably never hurt anyone in his life. And he took them to the cleaners, Bernie. It cost them a fortune. It was a very expensive lesson for the press. But you don't seem to have learned it. You've done your own hatchet job. On someone called Westwood. And what evidence do you have for this story? The gossip of some woman about whom you know nothing, except that she gave you a false name.'

Chastened, Bernie said, 'You're not going to run my story?'

'That's right. I'm not. You'll thank me one day. And let me tell you this: if I learn that you attempted to sell this to another paper, you'll be out of work. Do you understand?'

'So what are we going to do?'

'We are going to ring the police, Bernie. *You* are going to ring the police, so that at least you get some brownie points with them. You will give them all the notes you've taken.'

'I didn't take any notes. I recorded the conversation.'

'You... What? Did you get her permission? In writing?'

Bernadette shook her head.

'What got into you? Were you trying to commit professional suicide? Right; you ring the police and you give them your recording. You tell them that you realise that the recording is dynamite and, *of course* you wouldn't dream of printing the story, but you think they might find it useful. Then you ask – very politely, Bernie – for their guidance if any part of the story is usable by us. Do it now.'

* * *

Bernie knew that DCI Bill Blazeley was the senior investigating officer on the Cedric Bartholomew and Ali Badaan cases, and so he was the one she called. When she arrived at the police station, it was DI Susanna David who met her at reception, took the recorder from her, and thanked her with a warning. 'My understanding is that you recorded a conversation with another person with the intention of using that recording for gain but without obtaining the other person's permission. That is a criminal offence. I'm not going to ask the CPS to consider charging you. In fact, I'm not going to investigate the matter any further. But I am issuing you with this caution. You have committed an offence and if it comes to our attention that you have repeated this offence with someone else, you should expect to be prosecuted. Do you understand?'

Bernie nodded. 'Believe me, nothing you say is likely to match the bollocking I got from my editor. I've been given a crash course in journalistic ethics. You can take it from me, nothing like that will happen again.'

The half-smile on Susanna's face suggested that she was aware that Bernie's fingers were crossed, at least metaphorically, as she said this. 'Thank you for the recording. I'll let you have the recorder back as soon as we are done with it.'

'Yes. Actually, Inspector, I'd like to ask a favour.'

Susanna raised an eyebrow in silence.

'Yes,' said Bernie. 'When you've listened to what the woman on that tape has to say, will you let me know whether there is any part of it that you think it would be all right for us to print?'

The silence this time was prolonged as Susanna stared at the reporter. Then she said, 'Okay. If there's anything that won't harm our investigation, I'll tell you.' Then she said, 'By the way, is there anything you feel you need to tell us?'

When Bernie looked blank, Susanna went on, 'Jensen Bartholomew has been employing a firm of bodyguards since his brother was murdered.'

'Yes. I know. I mentioned that in my report of his brother's death.'

'So you did. But in your latest report, when you said that a man had been killed in the churchyard and that police believed his name to be Westwood, you didn't say that Westwood had been suspected of Cedric Bartholomew's murder. In fact, that has never appeared in any of your stories. When I listen to this tape, will I find a suggestion that Westwood killed Bartholomew?'

Bernie nodded. 'Yes. She says that.'

'And does she also say that Westwood killed Ali Badaan?'

Bernie shook her head. 'Listen to her. On the recording. She gives me Cedric Bartholomew's name as a taster. For any more, she wants two thousand quid.'

'I see. But you haven't had time yet to put that into *The Post*.'

'It's in the story I wrote. After I recorded that conversation. But the editor spiked it. He said we couldn't use it.'

'I'm glad that someone in your organisation has a proper regard for the law. When Cedric Bartholomew was killed, we assigned a Family Liaison Officer to Jensen Bartholomew.'

'I'm surprised he needed one. I mean, having hired a full-time professional bodyguard.'

'That's a common misconception, Bernadette. FLOs aren't appointed for the benefit of the family who suffered a loss. We're happy to let the family believe that, but the FLO is a policeman and he's there on police business. And just before you rang, Jensen Bartholomew's FLO told us that Mr Bartholomew had dispensed with the professional bodyguards.'

'Ah.'

'Yes. You've got that somewhat shifty look that I imagine everyone who has anything to do with you becomes used to, sooner or later. I'll ask you again: is there anything you feel you need to tell us?'

Bernie was looking at the floor. 'I rang Mr Bartholomew.'

'You told him that a man called Westwood was dead and you told him that we believed Westwood to be Cedric Bartholomew's killer.'

'I wanted to get a quote from him.'

'And did you?'

Bernie shook her head. 'He didn't even thank me for the news.'

'You've interfered in the conduct of a police investigation. And not for the first time. It's a very risky thing to do. It could get you into a lot of trouble. And you can take that as a formal warning.'

Susanna took the recorder upstairs to the incident room and sat down with Bill Blazeley and a civilian typist who was going to transcribe what was on it. They listened to the recording. Then they listened a second time, and then a third. Susanna said, 'What do you think, boss?'

Blazeley laughed. 'I think it's the biggest load of old cobblers I've heard since you told us what Del Theobald had to say about Westwood. Who is this woman? She admits she's not Becky Smith, but who is she? We need to follow up that story about the missing boyfriend with the Met. If the boyfriend's parents are as powerful as this woman suggests, they'll have a record of their visit to her. They'll know her name and they'll know who the boyfriend was, too. Get Marion to put all of that on HOLMES. But tell her you'll be the one talking to the Met. While you're talking to Marian, we need someone to find out who owns Jamaica House. And we need to pay the place a visit. I don't think we want to go in there shorthanded, if it really is inhabited by a dandy who feeds people to pigs. Take Rayann with you, but also take one of the DCs and two uniforms with tasers.' He looked up. 'Charlie. Good to see you here. Have you got news for us?'

'I've just come from Saint Mary's churchyard,' said the crime scene manager.

'Ah, yes. From the body of Thomas Westwood, according to what you found in his pocket.'

'Yes, sir. But not according to his fingerprints. We haven't got the DNA results yet, although I've asked for them urgently, but the fingerprints belong to someone called Dominic Carter.'

'Do they, indeed? Well, now – I suppose it's possible, since we'd never heard of Thomas Westwood, that Westwood is the name Dominic Carter has been going under. Thanks, Charlie. Susanna, one more thing we need Marian to log – who was Dominic Carter?'

CHAPTER 13

Before she left, Susanna called London. Of course she knew she wasn't going to get an immediate answer, but only she could start the process. Who was this woman the Metropolitan Police had called on to ask what had happened to her boyfriend? She didn't know how things worked inside the Met, what internal networks there were, but if that visit had been arranged at the behest of some wealthy, powerful person, there would be a record of it. The person she spoke to said they'd call her back. 'But it's unlikely to be tonight.'

'Of course. I'll give you my mobile number, so you can get me wherever I am.'

Then she rang Manchester police and asked a similar question. Someone had studied the CCTV recorded at Manchester Piccadilly railway station and then they'd spoken to the ticket seller to try to find out who had bought a ticket for a young woman travelling to London Euston on her own. That certainly was not something everyone involved would have forgotten. And then she went home.

Members of a major crimes investigation team don't get many interrupted evenings to themselves while looking for a murderer. They get even fewer as the number of deaths rises. Susanna David knew how lucky she was to get home that evening before eight. She also knew how lucky she was that her partner, Detective Superintendent Chris McAvoy, had reached a level of seniority at which he was almost always able to keep normal office hours, that he loved to cook, and that he was good at it. She said, 'If you had your time over, what would you choose? The police? Or the kitchen?'

'If it was the same me making the choice, it would be the police again because I had no idea in my teens that I'd enjoy cooking so much. I wasn't one of those kids who take over the job of feeding the family. But if I'd known then what I know now? I might well have got myself apprenticed to a chef. It's even crossed my mind, when I retire, to open a restaurant. But I won't – that's the kind of dream that should never be put into practice.'

'So what is it tonight?'

'Tonight we have braised chicken with tarragon, chervil and sun-dried tomatoes.'

'Sounds lovely.'

'When people first started talking about sun-dried tomatoes, I thought it was just one more fashionable trend that would disappear before long. But it isn't. There's a concentrated, long-lasting body and taste that you don't get any other way. I'll be dishing up in about twenty minutes.'

'That just gives me time for a quick shower.'

'And to pour us each a glass of wine.'

'I'll do that before I take the shower.'

'Good thinking.'

* * *

Nicola, too, was relishing an evening off, which in her case meant supper at her sister's house. Sasha's husband, Kevin, had a very high paid job in some obscure aspect of banking that Sasha professed not to understand. Whatever it was, it had taken him to Dubai for a conference, and Sasha was delighted after a day spent with their children to welcome Nicola for a meal. 'I wouldn't be without them for a moment,' she said. 'I love them to tiny little pieces. But I do so long for the time they'll be able to talk like adults.'

'It's a shame they're asleep,' said Nicola. 'I'd have liked to see my little nieces.'

'You need to get here a bit earlier for that, my dear sister. They are one and three years old and by this time of night I expect them to be in bed. Let me pour you a glass of something.'

'Not too much – I have to drive home.'

'Surely the police would let you go when they realise who they've stopped?'

'You must be joking. They'd charge me faster than they'd charge anyone else. Anyway, I need a clear head. We've got some very strange stuff going on.'

'Which I imagine you can't tell me about.'

'Not in detail. Sorry.'

Sasha nodded. 'You wanted to be a detective for as long as I can remember. Is it what you expected?'

'Yes, it is. And no, it isn't. Even in major crimes, we don't have enough people and everyone has to work far too hard. But at least we don't have to decide what we have time to work on and what we don't, like CID. We deal with murders and serious crimes where only a solution will do. Sometimes it takes time, but you can never walk away and leave something. But in CID every detective might have anything from twelve to more than twenty cases open at the same time and sometimes they have to say, "It's a pity, but we have to accept we are never going to catch the people who broke into that house, or sold those drugs, or mugged a poor old lady on the street and shook her up so badly she died a few weeks later.'

'Those are the things the press hammer you for.'

'Well, you can't blame them. That poor old lady almost certainly has children and grandchildren. We'd never get CPS to agree to a manslaughter charge even if we caught the mugger, but the family knows it was the mugging that killed her. And when they realise we aren't going to win justice for her, you can understand it if they think we aren't doing our job.'

'Especially if they see the police wasting their time investigating hate crimes.'

'Hate crimes are important, too, Sasha. You get people causing trouble because this woman is Jewish, that man is a Muslim, someone else is gay. Gay people, Muslims, Jews – they're all entitled to live their lives without being attacked because someone else doesn't like what they stand for. And that goes for black people and cross dressers, too. The world has changed from the one our mother grew up in.'

Sasha couldn't prevent herself from laughing. 'How did you know I was channelling her?'

'It's just the sort of thing she would say. The police shouldn't be wasting their time on oddballs. They should be looking after the interests of people like her. She doesn't realise, for a lot of people, oddballs means people like her. Has she been giving you trouble about me again?'

'You could say that. She doesn't understand why you want to do what she thinks of as such a dirty job – a *man*'s job. She thinks, if you found the right sort of man to marry you and look after you, you'd stop this foolishness, stay home and raise grandchildren for her. And she thinks, if

159

you won't look for the right sort of man yourself, it's my job to find him for you.'

'I'm sorry you have to put up with that.'

'Honestly, Nic, if it keeps the pressure off you, I don't mind. But let's eat.'

Later, when Nicola had eaten everything Sasha had placed before her, Sasha said, 'This right sort of man. I don't suppose…'

'I might find him for myself? I might. But we'd better face it. The man who would be the right sort for me…'

'Would not be the right sort for our mother.'

'It seems unlikely.'

'There's no one at work?'

'That's the difficulty, isn't it? At work has always been the most likely place to find your life partner, ever since women were allowed to join the paid workforce. But getting involved with a cop? Have you any idea what sort of hours they keep?'

'I've developed one, since you joined. What about that dishy oriental looking guy you work with?'

'Rayyan. I've been tempted.'

Sasha had not been subject to the same concerns as Nicola and, unlike her sister, had not confined herself to a single glass of wine. Her face was pinker than usual and now she scrunched up her eyes and opened her mouth wide. 'Nic! Tell me!'

'It didn't come to anything. It was last year, when we were looking into those killings by the two women. I went back to his one evening for pizza and beer.'

'Nothing happened?'

'Nothing. I've no idea whether he was willing, because common sense reasserted itself. I kissed him on the cheek, said good night, and went home.'

'No afterburn?'

'I'm not sure exactly what you mean by that, sister dear, but there's nothing going on between me and Rayyan. Which is probably the sensible option.'

'Sensible. Sensible isn't always the best choice in these matters. Does he know you were international standard in tae kwon do?'

'Probably. Most people at work do.'

'That probably puts him off trying anything. In case you bounce him off three walls and then make his arms into a pretzel. You might have to make the first move yourself. If you change your mind, that is.'

'I honestly don't think Rayyan is the kind of man to try anything. In any case, I must go. It's a big day tomorrow, and an early start. Thanks for a fabulous meal.'

* * *

Meanwhile, DC Theresa Pearson soaked in a deep bath fragrant with salts her mother had given her for Christmas and pondered the proposal she was about to make. She had known her motives were complex when she had told a surprised but very pleased Jamie that he was going to marry her. One, certainly, was that she didn't think she'd find another prospect who made her feel better – about herself or about him. Was that love? She wasn't entirely sure, though if you'd asked whether she loved her husband she would certainly have said yes, because that's what people did say unless they intended the marriage to end. Theresa had no such plan. But she'd also known that she wanted to become a detective – an ambition she had now fulfilled – and that Jamie would be happy always to be in uniform and to drive a police car. One of the things that meant was that his hours would always be that much more regular than hers. And, if you were going to be a parent, regular hours mattered. If the mother didn't have them, the father must. Was this the right time to introduce Jamie to her wish for children? Would there ever *be* a right time?

There were other things to think about. She'd already passed the sergeant's exam when she proposed to Jamie and she had every expectation of making the step up within the next two or three years. After that – how far could she go? Inspector? Certainly. She'd never doubted that she had what it took to get there. After that, politics came into it a bit as well as ability and being in the right place at the right time, but Chief Inspector might not be beyond her and Superintendent might one day turn out not to be a dream. Whereas Jamie, intelligent though he was, had no aspiration beyond constable. A lot of men would resent seeing their wife get that far ahead of them. Was Jamie such a man? She really didn't think he was. He knew all about her ambitions and he'd never shown any sign that they troubled him. And, of course, he was a few years older than her so he'd be leaving the force with a pension that much earlier. He could get a job in security, perhaps. Or even, if she was doing well enough, stay home, raise the kids and be a house husband. Someone to have dinner on the table when she came home, tired out after a hard day's detecting. To run her a bath. To look after her other needs.

She'd read that a survey by psychologists somewhere or other said that women who were the main breadwinners faked orgasms more often than women who weren't. Well, psychologists said all kinds of barmy things. You could make a good case for saying that you had to be more than slightly nuts to get into psychology in the first place. In any case, was faking it so bad? She'd done it herself on occasion, when she just hadn't been in the mood but she hadn't wanted to hurt Jamie's feelings. The male ego could be such a fragile thing.

She heard the doorbell ring and Jamie answer it. That was good; the pizzas had arrived. She got out of the bath and reached for a warm towel. Her mind was made up. There might never be a right time, but there was *the* time, and it had arrived.

When she got downstairs, Jamie had sliced the pizzas and poured himself a beer. He waved an empty glass in her direction. 'Want one?'

Yes, she said. Yes, she would like a beer. And when it was poured and they were both sitting down to start the meal, she said, 'Jamie. There's something I want to talk about.'

That conversation went on for some time. Babies were only the beginning – after that they had to talk about the extra space they'd need, and how much they had saved towards a deposit on a house, and what kind of house they could afford, and the fact that they'd also need enough fenced-in grass at the back for Jamie to play football with their offspring.

'That's if it's a boy,' said Jamie. Theresa's raised eyebrows told him, as they had told him several times in the past, that he had made a mistake.

'Girls play football, too, Jamie.'

He was about to laugh, but stopped himself in time. 'I'm sure a daughter of yours will.'

'And you will teach her.'

He poured more beer for both of them. 'I will, my darling.'

'So we are agreed? I should stop taking the pill? It's a joint decision? I don't want you to feel railroaded.'

'You can stop right away.'

'Good.' And then she started to tell him about the case and it struck her, as it had done many times before, that one part of the force could be completely taken up with whatever was concerning it at the time while another part knew nothing about it. Jamie had been aware of the murders – in fact, he was the one who had been sent to Saint Mary's churchyard and found the body that might belong to Westwood, might belong to Dominic Carter, might be someone else altogether – but he knew nothing of the enquiries they had been conducting. She had got as far as telling him about how the masked man who killed Cedric Bartholomew had peered into the lens to tell Jensen Bartholomew, "You're next," when Jamie said, 'Clever.'

'What do you mean?'

'Jensen. The brother who wasn't killed. Setting up cover like that. Clever.'

'Cover?'

'Well, wasn't it? You want to kill your brother and you don't want the police to suspect you, so you fake a threat against yourself. I'd call that clever.'

Theresa stared at him. Part of her wanted to say, "It's not about sudden flights of inspiration, Jamie. That's just for TV." And another part wanted to say, "Jamie, you are a genius." What she actually said was, 'Mmm. Maybe. But proving it is something else.'

CHAPTER 14

Susanna kicked off the briefing next morning by saying she'd had a call from a Chief Inspector in London who said he'd been very interested in her enquiry and he'd spoken to every likely police station and every likely special department. 'No one remembers an incident like this. No one. Of course, there's never a guarantee, but if you want my opinion, you've been sold a pup. It never happened.'

'So,' said Blazeley. 'What do we make of that? Are they covering for someone? Is it just bad record-keeping? Or is he right? Did Becky Smith, whoever she really is, make the whole thing up?'

'I'd be reluctant to come to that conclusion,' said Susanna, 'except that I've also had a call from Manchester. They have no record and no recollection of the CCTV incident at Manchester Piccadilly.'

'So,' said Blazeley once more. 'It could still be a cover-up, but if it is it's a joint effort by the Met and Manchester police. And knowing that Manchester have no higher opinion of the Met than any other force has, that's not a view I lean towards.

What was Becky Smith up to when she fed that yarn to Bernadette Spence?' A hand was raised among the assembled detectives, and Blazeley said, 'Yes, Tom. You have a view?'

'Sir. I spent a couple of hours going through the CCTV at Parkway Station. I've got a photograph of the woman calling herself Becky Smith when the journalist picked her up, and another one when she brought her back. I've had prints done and I'll pass them round.'

'Well done, Tom. But hold on – there are five prints here. And one of them is a man.' Excitement entered his voice. 'And one is a car. What's the story?'

'Yes, sir. There's no shortage of CCTV at the Parkway. The woman did not leave on a train. She went straight through the station, out the other side, and got into a Range Rover driven by that man.'

'In this picture, he's standing outside the Range Rover, smoking a cigarette.'

'Yes, sir. When the woman got into the car, the camera really didn't get a clear picture of the driver. So I tracked back on the CCTV and I got lucky because he got out of the car for a smoke and that's when we got the clear shot of him.'

'Tom, that's fantastic. Well done. And you say you got lucky, but the fact is you stuck with the job until it was finished. Is that definitely the index number of the car they left in?'

'Yes, sir, it is. And the car is registered to Sovereign Research. They have a Swansea address.'

'Better and better. Marion, a task for HOLMES: we need to know everything we can about Sovereign Research. Assign that task to Tom. Right. Who's next? Anna, you have something to tell us? You're looking a little shellshocked.'

'I may well be,' said the detective sergeant he was speaking to. 'I had to find out who Dominic Carter was and how his fingerprints came to be on record.'

'Yes? And you have?'

'I have, boss. Dominic Carter is a person of interest in a case currently being pursued by South Wales Police. He is also a director of Sovereign Research.'

A murmur went round the incident room. Detectives get used to the idea that nothing much is happening. That they are picking their way forward, one piece of information at a time. That they only have part of the picture, and not a large part at that. And then, from time to time, something happens that jolts the picture into a different shape. Often, what causes that jolt is that two pieces of information that had seemed unrelated to each other suddenly connect. This felt like one of those moments. Blazeley said, 'Tom. When you're looking into Sovereign Research, have Anna with you. Susanna, why don't we give these photographs to *The*

Post? Say that they are people we'd like to speak to. See what pops out of the undergrowth.'

'I'll speak to the Press Office, boss.'

'Yes. But have a word with Spence yourself. Tell her how much of the "story" Becky Smith told her she can print. I suggest just enough to get some ideas out there, see if anyone recognises something. And tell her she only has a 24-hour start and then we'll be circulating the pictures nationwide. Rayann, email those pics to wherever Del Theobald is being held on remand and ask if he recognises anyone. Does anyone else have anything?'

Theresa had been looking forward to this moment. She'd also been dreading it. Some of the detectives in this room had been doing the job for twenty years. She was a rookie. What she didn't want was to make a fool of herself. You didn't start the journey to Superintendent like that. And she was going to have a family. In fact, given what she and Jamie had got up to last night when they'd finished the beer and pizza and gone to bed, she might already be carrying the first seeds of that family. Nevertheless, she wanted to get this out into the open. She held up a hand.

Blazeley turned towards her. 'Yes, Theresa.'

'Sir. This is probably foolish, and in any case you've probably already thought of it, but...' She was aware that every face in the room was turned towards her. 'Sir. Nicola said something at a previous meeting and I can't get it out of my mind.' She could see the slight trace of a smile on Blazeley's face. But was he encouraging her? Or taking the mickey? She went on, 'What Nicola said was that, if the killer really intended to kill Jensen Bartholomew after killing his brother, he would have done it the other way round. Because killing Cedric Bartholomew in the way he did it put Jensen Bartholomew on notice that he might be in danger. And Jensen Bartholomew had all the money he needed to make sure he was heavily protected. Which he hadn't been before his brother was killed.'

'Yes. I remember. Go on.'

'The suggestion at that time, sir, was that whoever killed Cedric Bartholomew didn't really want to kill Jensen Bartholomew. What he wanted was to scare Jensen Bartholomew into handing something over – money, something else, who knows? But suppose that wasn't it, sir. Suppose it was Jensen Bartholomew who arranged for his brother to be killed. And he had the killer threaten him so that he wouldn't be suspected.'

Once again, a murmur was going round the incident room. Theresa could feel the meaning of that murmur. The others around her – her peers, but also her superiors – weren't making fun of her offering. They were weighing it. Considering it. And they weren't ruling it out. And nor was

Blazeley, because he said, 'It's a good point, Theresa. How can we test it?'

She'd prepared no answer to this. Thinking on her feet, she said, 'We need to know more about Jensen Bartholomew's business. We need to know whether Cedric Bartholomew still did things for him and, if so, what they were. And we need to know whether there was anything between the two brothers that would make Jensen want to kill Cedric.'

'And how can we answer those questions?'

'Ask Jensen Bartholomew?'

'I think that's exactly right. Susanna, I'd like you to brainstorm with Theresa, please. Plot out a line of enquiry with Jensen Bartholomew. And then the pair of you can go there and execute the plan. Let Rayann go to Jamaica House without you. Anyone else got anything to say?' When no hands went up, Blazeley said, 'Right! Let's get out there and get our jobs done. Whether it's Jensen Bartholomew or someone else, there's a killer roaming free and we need to get him off the streets.'

* * *

Susanna and Theresa spent some time in the interview room planning their approach to Jensen Bartholomew. When they had it straight, Susanna said, 'Right. Let's get on with it. Check which FLO is with him right now, call him on his radio and find out where Bartholomew is. Tell him we are on our way.' While Theresa was doing that, Rayyan was waiting for his armed escort to be assembled before visiting Jamaica House. He came to Susanna's desk. 'I've heard back from the screw who showed the photographs to Theobald. Theobald didn't recognise any of them.'

'We aren't really surprised, are we?'

'Not about most of them, no. But I slipped in a photograph of the body in Saint Mary's churchyard.'

Susanna sat upright. 'He didn't recognise that?'

'Not according to the screw.'

'Oh. So that means…'

'It means,' said Rayyan, 'that Dominic Carter is not Westwood. And it means that Westwood is still out there. We'd better hope Del Theobald doesn't find out. The poor guy will wet himself.'

* * *

The same information had reached the two men who had previously met in a London club to discuss Westwood. They were there again. Cantrell laid a photograph on the low table on which stood a pot of coffee, cream, sugar and almonds shelled, roasted and salted in the club's own kitchen.

'Do we know him?' asked the other man.

'His name was Dominic Carter. He is the one I sent to deal with Westwood.'

'What happened?'

'I would have described him as the most reliable man I knew in his line of work. Clearly, Westwood is even better than I gave him credit for.'

'What are the police doing?'

'That's what I'm worried about. They'll be trying to find out as much as they can about who Carter is. Or was, I suppose I should say.'

'Is that going to lead them to us?'

'Carter was already a person of interest to the South Wales police. I think we were dealing with that okay. But now…'

The other man took a handful of salted almonds. He rang a bell and, when a waiter arrived, he asked for a beer. Then he said, 'And bring it to me on the smoking terrace, please.' He waved his hand at the things on the table. 'Bring these, too.' He waited till the waiter had left and then said to his colleague, 'I know you don't indulge, Cantrell, but it's time you told me the whole story. And I think better with a cigar in my hand.'

* * *

It was break time for Jamie Pearson and his work partner and they were parked in a layby near a trailer that advertised hot food. The coffee there wasn't bad. Jamie said. 'My wife wants us to try for a baby.'

'You'd make a fabulous father, Jamie.'

Was that true? Would he be good as a father? He'd certainly put up no opposition when Theresa raised the question. In fact, if he gave it any thought, having children of his own had often been in his thoughts over the years. And when Theresa had suggested it, it had seemed very obvious and natural. As though it was obvious that there should be a new person in the world, and that he and Theresa should be its father and mother. And Jamie could see that he would have a special place in this child's life. Because, although Theresa hadn't mentioned it, the fact was that as a detective her hours were less regular than his. Which meant he, Jamie, would have to do the lion's share of the day-to-day parenting. Something else she hadn't mentioned was that he'd be retiring before her, and that she had ambitions to reach the higher ranks. Which were also the higher pay grades. He could even imagine bringing his retirement forward a little and becoming a stay-at-home father. The kind of father who stood at the school gates among all the mothers, waiting for his charges to be released to him. Maybe he'd mention that to Theresa some time. But maybe not – a lot of women wouldn't like the idea of being the main breadwinner. He didn't think Theresa was particularly like that, but you never knew.

A story had been going around a little while ago that women who were the main breadwinner faked orgasm more often than women who weren't, but that didn't trouble him. He'd never failed to satisfy Theresa. She'd never had to fake it. If she had, he'd have known.

He smiled. 'Do you think so?'

And then Control rang with urgent instructions, and the conversation was over, at least for the time being.

Have You Seen These People?

Bernadette Spence

Batterton police today asked for Post readers' help in identifying the people in this photograph. The woman pictured visited our offices and told me that her name was Becky Smith. But, sometime later, she said that that was not her name, though she refused to say who she really was. Police believe that "Becky Smith" has information that would help them identify the killer of Cedric Bartholomew and Ali Badaan, whose deaths have been covered in these pages this week. The man photographed drove "Becky Smith" away from her meeting with the Post in the car shown in the third photograph. Anyone with information that can help solve this mystery should contact Detective Chief Inspector Bill Blazeley or Detective Inspector Susanna David without delay.

They went to Jamaica House in two vehicles: Rayyan and Nicola in one and the two tasered-up uniformed constables in the second. They turned through the gate, drove to the house and then, instead of going straight on as Bernie Spence had with the woman calling herself Becky Smith, they turned into the wide gravelled space in front of the house and fanned out before the steps leading up to the main entrance. Rayyan told the uniforms to split up. One would go into the house with him and one would go round the back with Nicola.

The door was opened by a woman of about forty dressed in clothes that might have suggested she was a housekeeper and might have said she owned the place. When Rayyan held up his warrant card and introduced himself she settled that by saying, 'Mary Spilling. Housekeeper. Why are you here?'

Rayyan said, 'May we come in?' He rendered the question superfluous by walking through the door, the uniformed constable following. Mary Spilling said, 'Are you allowed to do that? Do you have a warrant? Shouldn't you have shown it to me?'

'We would need a warrant for a search,' said Rayyan. 'Unless we arrested someone connected with this house – then we could treat it as a crime scene and search every inch. We are here for general enquiries. Do you think we should get a warrant? Or arrest someone? Is there something we need to search for?'

At that point, they were joined by Nicola and the other uniformed constable coming from the back of the house, accompanied by another woman. Nicola said, 'This is Hannah Brian. She's a cleaner.' She held up her warrant card for Mary Spilling and gave her name. To Rayyan she said, 'There are two gardeners out the back.'

Rayyan said to Mary Spilling, 'Is there somewhere we can sit while I ask you some questions?' He turned to Hannah Brian. 'I'd like you to come too, please.'

The housekeeper led them into a large room in the front of the house. To Rayyan, the place had an institutional feel. It was more like a rundown hotel than a home, and more like a school than a rundown hotel although silence reigned and there were no children. The housekeeper gestured that they should sit. The sofas and armchairs, though far from new, were comfortable and in good shape. Rayyan's idea of the place was crystallising – like a rundown hotel, yes, but it had once been an above average home for people with taste and the money to indulge it. He said, 'Tell me about this house. Who lives here?'

Mary Spilling said, 'Before I tell you anything, I'd like to know why you are asking. What's this about?'

'It's a murder enquiry,' said Rayyan.

In his experience, those words usually got a response and that response usually spoke of some level of surprise and even shock. That didn't happen here, at least with the housekeeper. The cleaner put a hand to her mouth in a normal reaction to unexpected and unwanted news, but Mary Spilling didn't react at all. She said, 'Murder? Of whom?'

'A man called Cedric Bartholomew was strangled to death. Shortly after that, a man called Ali Badaan died when his throat was cut. That's all been in the press. It's in the public domain. Common knowledge.' He stopped there, and had the most interesting intuition – Mary Spilling was waiting for another name. She either knew, or wanted to know, about another death. Rayyan decided not at this point to mention the name of Dominic Carter. He said, 'Information received ties this house to a suspect in those murders. And I'm afraid that's all I can tell you. Now,

Jamaica House. Tell me who owns it and tell me who lives here. But please start with how long you have been here.'

The police get used to the many ways in which people react when questioned by the police. What struck Rayyan about Mary Spilling's manner was her unusual calmness. She said, 'I've been here for five years. I'm the only person who lives here permanently. From time to time, people come here to stay. We look after them, and they go. I don't know who owns the place – I'm employed by an agency, as is Hannah there, and the gardeners outside. You'd have to ask the agency who the owner is.'

'Then I have to start by asking you who the agency is.'

The housekeeper gave the details, and Nicola noted them on her tablet. It was a London address. 'Not local then,' said Rayyan. The housekeeper shrugged. Rayyan said, 'These people who come here to stay. What sort of people are they?'

'What sort? I don't know how to answer that. They're people.'

'But what do they come here for? Does someone arrange seminars? Is there a shoot? Are they here to walk? Fish? Surely, at the very least, you must know what kind of group they are, what sort of club they might belong to.'

The housekeeper sniffed. 'They don't come in groups; they come singly or in pairs.'

'Pairs? Married couples? Weekenders? What sort of pairs?'

'They are mostly men, and when there's more than one of them they have separate bedrooms. But usually there's only one.'

'Do you hire extra staff when you have people staying here?'

'If it's necessary. The agency does all that.'

'And how often does it happen?'

'Not often. I'm here on my own for probably ten months a year. Hannah lives out – she's a local girl.'

'You don't find it lonely?'

The housekeeper shrugged. 'My own company is enough for me.'

'Your accent suggests you're not local. How did you know this job was available?'

'It was offered to me.'

'Yes, clearly, but how? And who offered it?'

'I don't remember at this distance.'

Rayyan knew deliberate obstruction when he saw it. He also knew he had no power to change her attitude. Someone they didn't trust and couldn't identify had made an allegation they didn't really believe that someone living here had been involved in a crime that had either taken place in or ended in a pigsty in the gardens and might have happened and might not. He had no lever he could use to get her cooperation. He said, 'Where were you working before you came here?'

'Here and there. I moved around a little. I never really settled.'

'And yet you've been here five years.'

'I like it here.'

'Do you have any ID on you?'

Now he knew he'd hit something. She'd been unresponsive, but now she was hostile. 'I've told you who I am.'

'That's all right. If you don't want to show us anything, I'm sure the agency that pays you has your details. They probably also have a clearer recollection of where you worked previously than you seem to have.' He was aware that he was meeting hostility with hostility. If he was asked to justify the way he was speaking to someone who was suspected of no crime, he'd struggle to do it. Nevertheless, it produced a result. She opened her handbag and took out a driving licence. It confirmed that her name was Mary Spilling, it gave Jamaica House as her address, and it was possible to extract her date of birth from the DVLC's curious code. He handed it to Nicola, who photographed it on her tablet and handed it back to her.

There was a table near to the window. Rayyan was no expert, but he thought it likely that it could probably be sold for a great deal of money. He went to it and laid out some photographs he had brought with him. 'Could I ask you both, please, to take a look at these and tell me whether you recognise any?'

It was clear to him that the cleaner examined the photographs with a great deal more care and interest than the housekeeper, but both shook their heads. The housekeeper said, 'I've never seen any of them before,' and the cleaner, after a noticeable hesitation, said, 'Neither have I.'

Rayyan said, 'When was the last time you had anyone staying here?'

'About three months ago,' said Mary Spilling and when Hannah Brian looked as though she might be about to question that, the housekeeper silenced her with a glance. Rayyan said, 'Mrs Brian …?' Hannah shook her head. 'It was about three months ago.'

'Can you give me the person's name?'

'By all means,' said the housekeeper. 'He was called Barry Maitland. He stayed for six days. Why he was here, he didn't say and I didn't ask.'

Sometimes, a negative response to questioning can be overcome by changing the person asking the questions. Rayyan gave Nicola the quick look that meant, "Your turn," and she said, 'Does the name Thomas Westwood mean anything to either of you? Or just Westwood on its own?'

There was no doubt in the minds of either Rayann or Nicola; that name had been met with hostility by Mary Spilling and a touch of fear on the part of Hannah Brian. Hannah watched Mary as though taking a lead from her and, when Mary donned the look that said she was giving the question a good deal of serious thought and then said, 'No. I don't think I've ever heard that name,' Hannah also shook her head. 'Never.'

'We'll go and talk to the gardeners now,' said Rayyan. 'Mrs Brian, do you live in the village?'

The cleaner shook her head. 'My husband is a gamekeeper for Lord Bartland. We have a cottage on his estate.'

'Well, thank you. You've both been very helpful.'

When they got outside, Nicola said, 'Helpful? I take it that was a joke?'

Rayyan smiled. 'When you give all that stuff to Marion to put on HOLMES, make sure someone is tasked with getting an address for Hannah Brian's cottage. I want to speak to her without the housekeeper listening. And let's find out as much as we can about the housekeeper. Who is she, where did she come from, who did she work for before she came here, is anything known about her?'

CHAPTER 15

The SOCOs had finished at Jensen Bartholomew's office and Bartholomew and his staff were back at work. He raised no objection when Susanna and Theresa visited him there and they were shown straight into his spacious office. Bartholomew waved them towards a sofa beside a table in birdseye maple. He took a seat on a sofa on the opposite side. His secretary returned and put coffee and a plate of dark chocolate and ginger florentines on the table. She poured coffee for all three, handed each of them a plate and a linen napkin, and left the office, closing the door behind her.

Bartholomew smiled at the two detectives as if he hadn't a care in the world. 'What was it you wanted to ask me?'

As they had agreed in advance, Susanna led the way. 'Mr Bartholomew, you said immediately after the death of your brother that he had asked you three times to pay off large sums of money that he owed and that, the third time, you refused. Who did he owe the money to? And for what?'

Bartholomew's disquiet was clear. 'I wish I'd never said that.'

'We'd have known anyway,' said Theresa. 'It was mentioned on the recording of your zoom conversation with him.'

'So it was. And I expect that's why I said it. It felt disloyal to Cedric to tell you that. These are the side-effects of murder that you never think about until you're caught up in them.'

Theresa said, 'And the money? Where did it go?'

'I don't know. I gave it to him to deal with.' He passed a hand across his brow; if he wasn't feeling pressure, he was giving a good impression of it. 'Oh,' he said, 'I'm letting family loyalty get in the way of telling the truth. He was being blackmailed.'

'Blackmailed? Do you know for what, and who by?'

'He never named the person. He'd done something illegal and been found out.'

'See, the interesting thing about this, Mr Bartholomew, is that there is a puzzle over what your brother did with the money he had.'

'I didn't think he had any worth speaking of.'

'He certainly wasn't rich. But no one is allowed to starve in this country unless they choose to do so. Every month, your brother received six hundred and seventy pounds in universal credit. The council only charged him seven pounds a week for council tax because the government paid the rest. His rent was taken care of. He survived on sandwiches and pies that he bought from filling stations after they'd been marked down in price because they were past their due date. He rolled his own cigarettes, which he smoked sparingly, and he doesn't seem to have bought any alcohol at all. And yet, he had no money when he died. Nothing. Nothing in his pockets, nothing in the house, and only one pound in his bank account.'

'Don't, officer, please. I had so much and I didn't help him. You make me feel so bad.'

'I can't take responsibility for your feelings, Mr Bartholomew. But they are not the point. Where did the money go? We've been wondering that ever since he was killed, and now you tell us he was being blackmailed. We really do need to know who was blackmailing him and what hold they had on him.'

Bartholomew spread both arms in a gesture of bewilderment. 'If I could help you, I would. But I haven't the faintest idea.'

Susanna intervened. 'Has anyone ever tried to blackmail you, Mr Bartholomew?'

The look of bewilderment increased. Susanna's belief in it did not. 'Blackmail me? Why? How? For what?'

Theresa said, 'Your business is selling things to other countries and buying things from them. Have you ever had dealings with a country that companies in this country were not supposed to do business with?'

Susanna was beginning to be entertained by Bartholomew's ability to signal his emotions. The one on display now was amazement morphing gently into outrage. 'You mean, have I ever tried to break an embargo? I have not. And if anyone suggested I had, I would not pay money to keep them quiet. I would sue them.'

'Yes,' said Susanna. 'Of course. Did your brother still do any work for you? Of whatever kind?'

'He did not.'

'And when he was working for you, did he have specific countries that he dealt with?'

'Specific countries? All our import export business is outside the UK. That's what import and export means.'

'Yes,' said Susanna again. 'I wonder if you'd mind letting us have a list of every country your brother dealt with?'

'Well,' said Bartholomew. 'I suppose I can. It may take some time.'

'We'd rather it didn't,' said Susanna. 'When you're trying to find a murderer, especially one who has killed more than once, there's a certain amount of urgency involved. To catch the killer before someone else dies, apart from anything else.'

'Find a murderer? But I thought you'd arrested someone.'

'Now how did you know that, Mr Bartholomew?'

'That officer you placed with me. Even though I didn't want you to.'

'Your family liaison officer?'

'Yes. Him. He told me. He said you had someone under arrest. In fact, he said you would be charging him.'

Susanna made a mental note to remind the FLO that his job was to ensure a flow of information to the police from the person he was assigned to and not the other way round. She said, 'We do have someone in custody for one killing, that's true. But two other people have also been murdered…'

'Two others? My brother. Ali whatever it was. And… Of course – this chap Westwood. It was because he was dead that I was able to let the security firm go. But the story in *The Post* didn't say how he died. Are you saying he was murdered?' When he saw Susanna's nodded affirmation, he said, 'And if he was murdered…'

'There is at least one other killer at large,' said Susanna. 'Because the man we have arrested was already in our custody.' She let Bartholomew absorb the information. He certainly looked shocked. But was he? She said, 'So you see, Mr Bartholomew, we really do need as much information as we can get. In fact, I'd be grateful if you would allow our forensic accountancy people to look over your books. We are not HMRC and we wouldn't be looking for information we could pass to them about tax liability. What we'd want would be to see whether we could identify any customers who might have had a grudge against your brother.'

She watched Bartholomew closely. Although he struggled to keep his face impassive, a fight was going on behind it and she could guess what concerns he had. If he agreed to her request, who knew what they might find? But if he refused, would he be able to overcome the suspicions they would undoubtedly have? Suspicions that would almost certainly lead them to apply for a warrant to examine his accounts. However much he might dislike the idea, surely it was better to cooperate than to resist if they were going to get what they wanted anyway? And it seemed that Bartholomew's thinking mirrored her own, because after a long pause he said, 'I normally like to keep information like that confidential. The fewer people who know who we deal with, what we buy and sell, and what prices we agree, the better. I deal personally with one or two really sensitive accounts – I don't even let the staff here have the details – because my competition would love to get their hands on that information. But one has one's public duty. If you care to send someone here tomorrow, I'll make sure all the information is available. It may take time to pull together, so can we agree they won't come before eleven in the morning?'

Having achieved more than she had hoped, Susanna was happy to agree. A forensic accounting team was not, in any case, something she could call for off-the-shelf and it would probably take at least that long to assemble one.

* * *

In his London office, Cantrell was meeting the woman who had told Bernadette Spence she was called Becky Smith, though her brother called her Annabelle. 'Tell me: how many employees does Sovereign Research still have?'

'Only two, now that Dominic Carter is dead. Everybody else is hired through an agency.'

'And Carter was the only Englishman? The other two are both Iranians?'

'That's right.'

'Where do they live?'

'When they are in this country, we put them up in Jamaica House or one of the other safe houses. They don't much like it, so they come here as little as possible.'

'Too plain for the sophisticated Persian mind, I expect. Not enough gloss. Not enough high society. Not enough opportunities to flash their solid gold Rolexes. Staying home works well enough?'

'Oh, yes. They don't need to meet people. Their job is misinformation. Providing a smokescreen. Sleight of hand. This is the digital age – you can do all of that without ever leaving the comfort of your sitting room. And they do it well.'

'Of course they do. Upper-class Iranians are the most charming people in the world. Courteous, educated, outgoing, civilised. And I don't believe I've ever met a completely sane one. Be that as it may, I think the time has arrived to let Sovereign Research die. Keep your two Iranians on the payroll, but pay them through a different entity, find another way to route their input and keep them quiet until you have. No one is going to trace Sovereign's ultimate ownership?'

'Not according to my brother. And if you know anyone better at covering a trail, I'd like to meet them. And the accounts he filed for Sovereign are perfect. No case is ever going to be built on those, even though every single word is a lie.'

'Fine. South Wales Police are still investigating the company. Let them get on with it.'

'They'll find nothing in any records anywhere. And who are they going to talk to, if the only shareholders are in Iran and don't actually go by the names filed when the company was set up? We still have the Range Rover, of course. It's registered in Sovereign's name. I'll arrange to have it dumped and burned.'

'Excellent, Annabelle. I don't know what we'd do without you. And your brother, of course.' He took three files from his briefcase. 'I think your journalist contact will find these interesting.'

'I'll see to it. But I'm afraid she may have been to the police. The story she published was a very edited version of what I told her.'

'Probably her editor put a limit on what she could write. These will be too good to ignore. One last thing. Did the Iranians ever meet Westwood?'

Annabelle thought about that. 'No,' she said at last. 'We put him in The Lodge. I thought it was best to keep people apart, so far as we could. You know – as a general principle.'

'Good. I don't suppose it matters, but… Good.'

When Annabelle had left with the files, Cantrell raised a finger to summon a waiter. 'A gin and tonic, please. And some of your wonderful salted almonds.'

'Certainly, sir.'

Cantrell murmured, 'Ayatollah once. Ayatollah twice. Khomenei times aya gotta tollah?'

'Quite so, sir,' said the waiter.

CHAPTER 16

HOLMES had been updated, tasks had been distributed, time had been allowed for progress to be made and now DCI Bill Blazeley was opening another briefing session. Susanna was there, but she had told Theresa to take the lead in reporting their meeting with Jensen Bartholomew. The girl needed practice, and it would build her self-confidence.

When Theresa was done, Blazeley said, 'I've spoken to the Super. A forensic accounting team will be at Bartholomew's office at one this afternoon.'

'Let's hope he doesn't try to hide things,' said Rayyan.

'In some ways, I hope he does,' said Blazeley. 'These guys are mustard. If he doesn't show them everything, they'll know. What's next?'

In quick succession they were given the address of Hannah Brian's cottage and told that the jacket Ali Badaan had been wearing when he'd been so savagely murdered had been traced to a department store in town. 'They lost three of them altogether, all from the stockroom. They've installed CCTV there and they think they've identified a young guy called Sean Mahoney as the thief. He was working there. The address they have for him is in Dryden Close. He's disappeared and uniform are trying to find him.'

'I don't suppose there's anything there for us,' said Blazeley. 'Somebody nicked a jacket and sold it to Badaan – there's probably no connection between the jacket and the killing. Still, we'd better talk to Mahoney when he's picked up. Anyone else?' A hand went up, and Blazeley said, 'Marilyn? What have you got?'

'I talked to the agency that hires people for Jamaica House. Mary Spilling was hired as housekeeper five years ago. She came with glowing references from her job as housekeeper at the Marlborough Club in London. What is particularly interesting about that is that the Marlborough Club amalgamated with the Windham Club in 1945 and closed altogether in 1953.'

'So,' said Blazeley, 'she got her job with forged references. I'd like to think that was enough to call Jamaica House a crime scene and send the SOCOs in there, but it probably isn't. Shame. Still, Susanna, I think that's good cause to go back to Jamaica House and give Ms Spilling a harder time than you have so far.'

'I think so, boss,' said Susanna. 'But perhaps we'll hold back on that until after I've talked to Hannah Brian without

Spilling being there. I don't think it will be hard to get Hannah Brian to tell us whatever it is she knows.'

* * *

Bernadette Spence walked into her editor's office and slapped three files onto the desk. He looked up. 'What have we here?'

'These files appear to belong to the law firm, Patel and Mayfield. But that isn't who brought them here. Becky Smith dropped them off.'

'What did she say about them?'

'Nothing. She said she couldn't stay. She said I'd find them interesting.'

'And do you?'

'Oh, yes. What they say is that Cedric Bartholomew circumvented American embargoes on trade with Iran.'

'Cedric. Not Jensen?'

'Not according to these documents. Cedric Bartholomew appears to have been acting off his own bat.'

'And the files belong to Patel and Mayfield? Don't they specialise in immigration? Getting permission for people to stay in this country who don't necessarily have everything the Home Office requires?'

'They do. And something else Cedric appears to have been up to was getting permission to stay, and even British passports, for people who didn't qualify. In some cases, for people we might really think we didn't want here.'

'You know you should give those straight to the police?'

'I know I expected you to tell me that. And I know I will give them to the police. Probably. But before I do that, I'd like a chat with Patel and Mayfield. And I'd like you to tell me that you approve of that way of doing things.'

'If things turn to rat shit, you want me there in the prison cell with you.'

'It won't come to that. Don't be so melodramatic. Do I have your authority to talk to Patel and Mayfield, or don't I?'

'You won't show them the files?'

'Of course not. I assume these files were stolen. The lawyers would want them back.'

The editor sat in thought. Then he said, 'Go ahead. I'll write you a note giving you my blessing.'

'Thanks, boss. I knew there was a human being hidden in there somewhere.'

'But when you've talked to them, the files go to the police. Without delay.'

* * *

Christina Mayfield's first response when Bernadette Spence arrived at the offices of Patel and Mayfield was cautiously welcoming. 'Ms Patel isn't here. But the press can help draw public attention to some of the grotesque injustices suffered by refugees who flee to this country in fear of their lives. Tell me what you want to know.' But when Bernie had done that, Christina Mayfield's attitude changed. She picked up a phone and began to key something into it.

'What are you doing?' asked Bernadette.

'I'm telling Adina – that's Ms Patel – that she'd better get back here. If she can't, I'm afraid our conversation will have to wait until she can.'

'That would be a pity,' said Bernie. 'I've already written a large part of the story and my editor says it will be in this afternoon's edition, come what may. I told him that running the story without your input would be unfair on you – but you know what editors are. Well, perhaps you don't, but I can tell you there is little trace there of the milk of human kindness.'

Christina gritted her teeth. 'I hear you, Ms Spence, and I understand the threat you are making.' She was staring at the screen of her phone. Then, muttering beneath her breath something Bernie was pretty sure was an oath, she pressed the call button and held the phone to her ear. 'Adina. I know you're busy. I wouldn't have sent my message if it wasn't urgent. I've got someone from *The Post* here.' A short pause and then, 'Yes, of course I could say that, but we'd regret it and so would our clients.' Another pause. 'She knows about Cedric Bartholomew's embargoed transactions. She hasn't said so, but I'm pretty sure she's seen the stolen files.' Pause. 'Thank you. I'll tell her you're on your way.' She put down the phone. 'She isn't far away – she should be here in about twenty minutes. I'm going to put you back into Reception and get you some coffee.'

When she had walked Bernie back into the small reception area and before the receptionist had asked how Bernie took her coffee, Christina walked towards the back of the building and disappeared.

It was just under twenty minutes before the door swung open and a livid-looking Adina Patel strode into the building. Ignoring Bernie, she said to the receptionist, 'Is Christina in our office?'

The receptionist shook her head. 'No, she's…'

'All right. I know where she is.' And she marched in the same direction as the one Christina had taken.

The receptionist smiled at Bernie. 'Smoking is not allowed anywhere in this building. But Ms Mayfield sometimes uses the yard at the back.'

Bernie felt a certain satisfaction that she had caused one of the partners to need a cigarette. If she was smoking, she probably felt under stress. And stress could make people talk. When the two partners returned, Christina Mayfield was a little shamefaced and Adina Patel looked furious. As they marched into the office that, it seemed, they shared, Adina turned to Bernie. 'You. Get in here.' Her first question, before Bernie had even taken a seat, was, 'Where did you get your information from?'

Bernie knew she faced a crossroads here. Allow this woman to dominate the conversation and she'd get nowhere. Come out all guns blazing and she just might snare a little gem she could use. She said, 'I'm afraid you don't understand how press interviews work, Ms Patel. I ask the questions; you provide the answers. Of course, you don't need to – but I have enough to run a story that Patel and Mayfield have withheld from the authorities information about illegal trade transactions being arranged by someone right here in this city. I came to offer you the opportunity to put your side of the story. If you don't want to take that opportunity…'

'Trade with Iran, other than for certain financial transactions, is not illegal in Britain.' The words were snapped out; Adina Patel's dislike for Bernie and her approach could not have been clearer.

'No,' said Bernie, 'it isn't. But Cedric Bartholomew facilitated the sale to Iran of American technology. America has made transfer to Iran of the kind of technology he sold illegal. If that got out, and it was clear that the British authorities had done nothing to prevent those sales, America might extend to this country trade restrictions it has applied to others. And if that isn't enough, what Cedric Bartholomew also did was to enable prohibited persons in Iran to bypass the financial restrictions that are enforceable in this country.'

She could see Adina Patel pondering her options. Nothing changed in the woman's expression as she stared at Bernie, but behind those dark brown eyes a series of ideas were being examined and, one by one, thrown back where they came from. At length, Adina said, 'Three files were stolen from this building. If you have them, you are guilty of handling stolen goods, knowing or believing them to be stolen, which is an offence under Section 22 of the Theft Act 1968.'

Bernie smiled. 'Yes, and that's exactly why the files are currently on their way to Batterton police station. We've already given the police information that came into our possession about the murder of Cedric Bartholomew. *The Post* is a law-abiding institution.'

'Perhaps. But the fact that you are here means that you wish to blackmail Christina Mayfield and me. And that is an offence under Section 21 of the same act.'

'You're being silly, Ms Patel.' She saw the rage building in Adina and it gave her pleasure, because angry people make mistakes and say things they shouldn't. She said, 'But if you want to be silly, that's your privilege.' She stood up.

'I'll tell my editor that you're not interested in having your side of the story heard.'

Christina Mayfield rested a hand for a moment on Adina Patel's arm. She leaned forward. 'I suggest we put behind us everything that's been said so far and start again. Ms Spence... Bernadette... May I call you Bernie? Why don't you tell us what you'd like to leave here with? And then we'll tell you what we'd like to leave with. And let's see if we can't arrive at some sort of consensus.'

Adina Patel sank into a chair. She was a picture of fury, but she seemed ready to let her colleague lead the conversation. Bernie said, 'The story we run will say that Cedric Bartholomew was involved in a number of cross-border transactions that could have brought serious consequences to this country as a result of infringements of American law. It will also say that Cedric Bartholomew obtained money by arranging for visas and, in some cases, British passports, to be given to people who were not entitled to them and, in some cases, whose intentions towards this country were extremely hostile.'

Adina Patel was unable to remain silent. Although Christina Mayfield once again reached out a hand to calm her, Adina shook it off. 'That was the fault of the government of this country. The person you should be speaking to is the Home Secretary at the time Border Force activities were subcontracted to third parties. British Embassies in some countries lost the right to check applications for visas and passports. That right was handed over – for a fee – to third party agencies. What do you think happens when someone with no allegiance to this country is able to decide who should be granted British passports and who should not?'

'I have no idea,' said Bernie, who in fact had a very good idea but wanted to hear what Adina Patel would say.

'You have no idea. Well, Ms Spence, I have a very clear idea indeed. The British passport is given to the person prepared to pay a significant sum to the person at the agency as a bribe. And it is not given to anyone not prepared or unable to pay that bribe. The question of whether the person is a fit person to be allowed into this country receives no consideration whatsoever. And no one with even the vaguest understanding of how things are done in the Middle East, in Asia or in Africa would be surprised at that.' She was shaking when she finished speaking. 'And now you have achieved your aim, Ms Spence. Because you have got me to say something I would have preferred not to say. And you have our files, and so you have the evidence that we knew what was going on and did nothing about it.'

'Yes,' said Bernie, her voice calm as she realised the scale of what she had won. 'For the benefit of our readers, would you mind explaining why you did nothing?'

There was silence from both lawyers. Then Christina Mayfield said, 'We did do something. We sought to use what we knew to help our clients survive in the hostile environment that Britain represents for migrants with no money and nothing to sustain them but the knowledge that return to the place they came from means death.'

'You blackmailed Cedric Bartholomew to raise money to help your clients.'

'No comment,' said Christina.

Bernie looked at Adina. 'No comment,' said Adina. 'And why do you concentrate on Cedric? What about Jensen Bartholomew?'

'The brother? He isn't mentioned in the files.' When she saw the look exchanged by the two lawyers, she said, 'Should he be? Have the files been doctored?'

The expression on Adina Patel's face now was one of despair. 'No comment.'

Bernie stood up once more. The two lawyers were on the verge of tears. Christina said, 'You have us in the palm of your hand. You have the power to end our professional careers. You could even send us to jail.'

A subdued Adina said, 'I'm sorry, Christina. I never could control my temper.'

CHAPTER 17

When Bernie had written her story, she pressed the button to send it to the editor. A few minutes later, he demanded her presence. He pointed at the screen. 'What the hell is this?'

Bernie had been really pleased with what she'd written. She said, 'What's wrong with it?'

'Bernadette. Have you had a sudden burst of morality? Do you think a reporter who worries about hurting other people has a future? What were you trying to achieve here?'

Bernie took a deep breath. 'I wanted to get across the idea of what had been going on without costing two women their professional livelihood.'

The editor stared at her, long enough that she began to wilt. 'Bernadette,' he said again, and she knew she was in trouble because when she was in trouble was the only time he used her full name. 'Those decisions are not for the likes of you and me. The Law Society will decide whether they can go on practising. The Crown Prosecution Service and a court of law will decide whether they should remain free. Neither of those things is up to you. Your job is to present all of the facts in a way that will allow *The Post* to achieve its only objective. What is our only objective, Bernadette?'

She swallowed. 'To sell papers.'

'To sell papers. To which end we tell the story in the way our readers want. A way that will allow them to raise their hands in horror and say, "Not in my name!" A way that will allow companies to look at our circulation and know that we are a safe home for their advertising budget. If I had wanted the kind of story you have written, I could have got a sixth former from Batterton Academy to write it. This is not a Bernie Spence story. A Bernie Spence story is written to get people riled up. To get them demanding to know how something could have happened and who they can hold responsible. A Bernie Spence story has people writing to their MP demanding that something be done. Rewrite this story sailing as close to the wind as you can without risking a lawsuit. Turn it into a Bernie Spence story.'

Usually, Bernie loved her job. At this moment, she hated it. When she sat down at her keyboard, her mind was full of the two women whose misbehaviour she was about to reveal, and the faceless refugees who would suffer as a result. But she told herself there was no point in refusing to write the story. The editor would only get someone else to do it. And Bernie wasn't going to let anyone else's by-line appear on a story as big as this.

Who Ordered Cedric Bartholomew's Murder? And why?

Bernadette Spence

Files passed to The Post suggest that the roots of Cedric Bartholomew's murder go deeper than the police may have suspected. Batterton law firm Patel and Mayhew had established that Bartholomew had conspired with parties unknown to sell advanced American technology to Iran, contrary to American law. He had also conspired to obtain British passports for people no responsible citizen would wish to see take up residence in this country. And what had Patel and Mayhew done with this knowledge? Had they handed the files to the police, as every normal moral consideration would require? No: instead, they had kept quiet and blackmailed the unfortunate Cedric Bartholomew, taking every penny he had in order to finance their operations which, at heart, are concerned with carrying on Bartholomew's work. They seized on the knowledge of Bartholomew's wrongdoing to underwrite protests, demonstrations and appeals against lawful decisions to refuse permission to stay to those whose presence in this country is considered contrary to the interests of the British people. The Post has now done what Patel and Mayhew failed to do, and provided the police with the files they need to protect our civilisation against those who would destroy it.

This time, when she hit the Send button, she got a different response from the editor. 'Well done, Bernie. An excellent job. And now I suggest you get those files into the hands of Bill Blazeley or Susanna David post-haste. They'll be reading this story later today, and it's not in your interests to have that happen before you have demonstrated your good citizenship and collaboration.'

'*My* interests?'

'Certainly, my dear. Yours among others. And when you've done that, get along to Jensen Bartholomew's office and find out what he has to say about his brother's shenanigans.'

* * *

Hannah Brian was visibly unhappy when Rayyan and Nicola knocked on her door. 'What do you want? Why are you here?'

Rayyan said, 'May we come in?'

Jamaica House had been a place of faded luxury, with furnishings that had once cost a great deal of money. The Brians' cottage was nothing like that. These people got by on the little they had – but the air of pride, of making the most of not very much, of looking after your home and yourselves, was striking. Rayyan got straight to the point. 'Mrs Brian, I wanted to see you on your own because it was fairly clear to me that there were things you didn't feel able to say when the housekeeper was present.'

They had scarcely noticed the man sitting motionless at the table, a mug of tea in front of him. It occurred to Rayyan that being able to make yourself almost invisible was probably an advantage in a gamekeeper. A sort of camouflage, automatically adopted as he looked around to see what, and who, was there. But now the man spoke. 'Tell them, Hannah. You owe Mary loyalty, but not to the point of lying or covering things up.'

His wife said, 'Living out here, jobs aren't easy to come by. We can't afford for me to lose this one.'

Rayyan said, 'Mrs Brian, I understand your reluctance to offend your employer. But in the last resort…'

'… In the last resort,' interrupted Hannah's husband, 'the most Mary Spilling can do is fire you. If you keep secrets from the police, you can end up in jail.'

Hannah slumped into a chair. 'What do you want to know?' Rayyan spread out on the table the same photographs he had shown at Jamaica House. 'When I showed you and Mrs Spilling these photographs, you both said you didn't recognise any of them. You also both told me that the name Thomas Westwood meant nothing to either of you. Do you want to change either of those statements?'

All of Hannah Brian's body language said she was deeply unhappy. She said, 'I need to change both of them.'

'Good. Take this in your own time. I know it's hard. But tell me what you weren't able to tell me before.'

From the photographs, Hannah chose the one of the woman they only knew so far as Becky Smith. 'I've never asked who the owners of Jamaica House are. It never seemed important. But this woman either is one of the owners or works for them.'

Rayyan felt the happiness that comes from real progress. 'Do you know her full name?'

'No, but Mary called her Annabelle.'

'She knew her?'

'I got the impression they were old friends. Annabelle would come from time to time, and she usually brought someone with her. Someone who would stay with us for a while.'

'Do you know who any of those people were?'

Hannah shook her head. 'No. Sorry. They were often foreign, but I've no idea where they came from. I mean, they weren't French, or Italian, or German, because I'd have recognised some of the words they used even if I don't speak those languages. When they spoke to me or Mary, they spoke the most beautiful English, but with a foreign accent. But when they were on their own, they spoke in their own language.'

Rayyan tapped a finger on the photograph of the man who had been shot in the churchyard. 'How about him?'

'Oh, yes. When Mary said it was about three months since the last visitor, I was about to say something because the last visitor was actually that man in your photograph. He was here about three days ago. But I could tell Mary didn't want me to say anything.'

'How did he get here? Did Annabelle bring him?'

'Yes, she did. And Mary told me that he would be staying for three nights, and Annabelle would come today and take him away. But he went out after the first night and never came back.'

'You didn't get his name?'

'When Mary talked to me about him, she just called him "the visitor." But I heard Annabelle introduce him to her as Mr Carter.'

'Thank you, Hannah, that's very helpful. When we were at Jamaica House, I asked if the name Westwood meant anything and you both said it didn't, but I wasn't convinced.'

'I've never met anyone by that name. But I did hear mention of Westwood when Annabelle was introducing Mr Carter to Mary.'

'But no one by that name has ever lived here?' When Hannah shook her head, he said, 'One last question. Do you think it's possible that anything may have been fed to the pigs in the pigpen that should not have been?'

He saw Hannah relax. Clearly, this was not a question that troubled her. 'Not in the time I've been there, and that's a lot longer than Mary Spilling because I worked for the people who had the house before. There haven't been pigs at Jamaica House for twenty years.'

When Rayyan and Nicola stood up to leave, Hannah said, 'You won't tell Mary I told you these things? I honestly can't afford to lose this job.'

'Don't worry, Mrs Brian. We will have to speak to Mary Spilling again, and we will have to challenge her on things she has said that weren't true, but we'll make it clear that our information came from elsewhere. You won't be mentioned.'

They were at the door when the gamekeeper said to his wife, 'Do they know about the Lodge?'

Rayyan raised an eyebrow. 'The Lodge?'

Hannah said, 'It's in Pinkline. Just outside the village. I went there once, just after they'd bought it, but I've never been asked to go since. But I know Mary looks after it as well as Jamaica House.'

'Thank you,' said Rayyan. 'Thank you very much.'

CHAPTER 18

Bernadette Spence did as her editor had instructed, and drove to the Bartholomew Group headquarters. Against all her expectations, Jensen Bartholomew agreed to give her five minutes, so long as she did not attempt to record the conversation. She would later wish he had refused to see her.

She said, 'Mr Bartholomew. When I interviewed the two lawyers at Mayhew and Patel, they expressed surprise that the documents in the files I had been sent referred only to your brother Cedric. They seemed to believe that you should also have been mentioned there. Do you have anything to say about that?'

It would have taken someone much less sensitive than Bernie to fail to see the hostility that passed briefly across Bartholomew's otherwise condescending features. 'No,' he said. 'I have no comment at all. I can't imagine what they were talking about.' He leaned forward. 'And I shall give you some advice, Ms Spence. If I were in your shoes, I would know that pursuing that line of enquiry might land me in difficulty. And now your five minutes are up. Let me walk you to the door and see you off the premises.'

When Bernie had left, Jensen went back into his office, closed the door, and made a call on the phone he kept for his own use and paid for himself. He hadn't come this far, hadn't arranged what he had and told the lies he'd told, to be exposed by a nosey journalist.

* * *

Susanna wasn't expecting to hear from the forensic accounting team any time soon, so it came as a surprise when DS Maisie Bertrand approached her desk. 'Maisie. You found something already?'

'I've found some things that suggest Bartholomew hasn't shown us everything. We wondered how you want to play it – do we confront him, do you want to do that yourself, or do we let it ride for now?'

'What hasn't he shown you?'

Maisie smiled. 'We don't know – he hasn't shown it to us.'

'Then how…?'

'If you want to cut your tax bill by fooling HMRC, the most important thing you have to do is to be consistent.'

Susanna smiled. 'I'll try to remember that.'

'It won't help you, Susanna. Or me. Our tax is deducted at source. But someone like Jensen Bartholomew and a company like the Bartholomew Group decide how much tax they are going to pay. It isn't that simple, obviously – their accounts have to be audited by a supposedly independent firm of accountants, and it's the accountants who say how much tax should be paid, but they do it on the basis of information provided by their client, the company. If you suddenly show a big reduction in taxable profits, HMRC will almost certainly decide to put you under the microscope. But if there's no sudden cut, the assumption will be that everything is going on as it should. Oh, they'll check you over from time to time, but they'll always be making that underlying assumption that you're not doing anything you shouldn't. That's what I mean by being consistent. And HMRC are desperately short of staff, and the staff they do have are demoralised. Partly because they have too much work to do, partly because they have no idea when the next round of redundancies will be announced and whether they'll be included, and partly because they don't have the training they need to be really forensic in their work.'

'Which is where you come in.'

'I hope so. I qualified as an accountant, spent three years with an auditing firm and the next fifteen with HMRC.

They made me redundant and the police offered me a job. Here I am. And what I'm tasked with really is forensic. My job is to see when things don't add up.'

'And they don't add up at Bartholomew Group?'

'One of the things I do is ratio analysis. In this case, I've been looking at how much it costs Bartholomew Group to make a sale. It varies country by country, but only to a certain extent. It's possible to say that, within certain limits, every hundred thousand pounds of sales to any given country costs a given amount. One of the things Jensen Bartholomew has been very good at is keeping that ratio steady year after year after year. And I've looked back at the company before Jensen took over and his father was every bit as regular. But then I compare Bartholomew Group's cost of sales with what happens in other companies audited by firms I trust. And they all show a lower cost of sales than Bartholomew Group.'

'I'm sorry, you're losing me.'

'Either Bartholomew Group is claiming costs it hasn't actually incurred – which is difficult – or it isn't reporting all the sales it's making. But it does declare enough sales and enough profit to keep the tax man happy.'

'Surely those missing sales will be in the bank account.'

'They'll be in a bank account, certainly. But which bank? In which jurisdiction?'

217

'You think they are hiding money in a tax haven.'

'I think it's extremely likely.'

'You said other companies audited by firms you trust. You don't trust Bartholomew Group's auditors?'

'I trust them about as far as I could throw a grand piano.'

'What do we do?'

'That's the difficult bit. Isn't it? I could ask Jensen Bartholomew the question. I could ask his auditors. In either case, I'd be warning them about my suspicions. And would I get honest answers?'

'It seems unlikely.'

'We'll keep looking, Susanna. But the purpose of this meeting was to let you know where we've got to, and what we think is happening.'

* * *

Bernie Spence drove back to The Post's building. She knew she'd just been warned off – threatened, in fact. It was by no means the first time someone had tried to get her to drop an investigation and she usually treated such incidents as part of the job of being an investigative reporter, so why was she now feeling so nervous? She checked her rear-view mirror constantly, but there was no sign that anyone was following her. When she got back to the office, her normal state of mind had reinstated itself. If you were a journalist, you asked questions. That's what you did. When the person you were asking didn't like the questions, you might occasionally be threatened. Over the course of her career, that had probably happened to her two dozen times. None of the threats had ever been translated into action, and nor would this one be. She sat at her desk and looked at the Post-it notes stuck to her screen. She got lots of these every day. Most were a waste of her time, but you just never knew when you were going to strike gold, and so she went through each one with care.

But, this time, there was nothing there.

* * *

Blazeley was going through HOLMES when he found an item that interested him. 'Why wasn't I told about this?'

Marion looked at him in surprise. 'The Automatic Number Plate Recognition message? I sent you a text.'

Blazeley looked at his phone and smacked his forehead with the palm of his hand. 'I'm sorry, Marion. I should have realised you wouldn't miss something like that. My mind must have been elsewhere.' He looked around the incident room. Most of the MCI team were out. To those who were present he said, 'Listen up. We'll cover this again at this evening's briefing, but the car that took the woman calling herself Becky Smith away from the Parkway station was picked up an hour ago by ANPR.' He went and stood by the large-scale map of the area. 'It was first seen on this A road here. Then it disappeared, presumably on minor roads where there are no cameras, and then it was seen on this A road. And then it disappeared again.' He pushed four large pins into the map. 'As it has not yet re-emerged, the assumption is that it is parked somewhere inside that area. We'll be notified if it moves and enters an A road. Marion, get Control to put unmarked cars here, here, and here. Give them the make of the vehicle and the index number. No car leaves their post until their replacement is in position. If anyone sees that car they are to follow it and they are to identify Control immediately and Control are to ring me, also immediately. And that applies at whatever time of the day or night the sighting may be.'

Marion said, 'Do you want them to stop the car?'

'Only if they think they've been spotted. What I'd really like is to find out where it goes.'

* * *

The three files stolen from Patel and Mayfield were sitting on Susanna's desk. She'd only got them because Bernie had left them at the front desk with her name on them. She'd glanced at the contents and seen that the man they implicated was Cedric Bartholomew, but got no further. Then someone placed a copy of *The Post* on her desk and, when she'd read Bernie Spence's column, she called Control. 'Send someone to the offices of Patel and Mayfield and tell them to bring the two partners back here. Arrest them if they don't agree to come willingly. Say we want to talk to them about allegations of blackmail. I want them held downstairs, out of contact with each other, until we are ready to talk to them.'

It was at that point that Rayyan and Nicola returned with news of the conversation they'd had with Hannah Brian.

CHAPTER 19

Jenny Frobisher's phone rang. Not the phone number she gave to journalists, friends and selected members of the public. This number was given to very few people. The party whips had it. The Prime Minister's office also had it – the PM had never called her on it yet, but you never gave up hope. The number that appeared on the screen was not one she recognised. When she answered, a voice that she very much did recognise said, 'Your husband has been sleeping on the job.'

'I'll tell him to call you.' And she put the phone down. Whatever the caller had to say, Jenny was determined later to be able to say truthfully that she knew nothing about it. Ambitious MPs needed to be very careful who they allowed to speak to them and what they let those people say. There was always some muck-raking journalist or political opponent ready to ask those risk-laden questions, What did you know? And when did you know it? A politician in a constituency where Bernadette Spence was a journalist learned about muck-raking very quickly. As for political opponents, Jenny had no shortage of those – in the opposition and, more actively, within her own party.

She went from the room she used as an office to the one Harold used for the same purpose. 'Please call Cantrell. It sounds urgent.'

'Right. Did he say what it's about?' But his wife had already left the room.

Westwood was restless. It wasn't a new feeling – in what now seemed the long ago, when he was an elite soldier fighting for a cause he believed in, restlessness had been normal. A sign that things were coming together and he would soon be back in the only mode he really felt comfortable in: making things happen. Responding to the unexpected, smoothing out obstacles and overcoming risk. Like the men in Housman's epitaph on an army of mercenaries, who saved the sum of things for pay. He'd liked that poem as a boy, dreaming about the great things he could do when school was over and he was free to go out into the world and change it. He never overlooked Housman's final words on those men: that they took their wages and are dead. Westwood's dreams of glorious feats of arms always ended in an equally glorious death, fêted in the style of Kipling, a poet he revered even more than Housman.

But he hadn't died. He'd obeyed orders, killed without compunction when told to do so – targets who deserved to die, that went without saying – and then budgets had been cut, the regiment had been butchered by Whitehall bean counters as it never had been by any enemy in the field and he'd been offered training for civilian life. As if civilian life was ever going to have any use for him. Or he for it.

He respected those who could make the change. They had done what he was unable to do.

Ehmed had been a subsistence farmer living hand to mouth in Iraqi Kurdistan and expecting no change. But then George Bush had decided that Saddam Hussein was an affront to liberal democracy and a danger to Americans and had to be removed. In the buildup to war, the right kind of people needed to be got through the home land of the Kurds and into Iraq itself to team up with fifth columnists there. Ehmed and people like him were prepared, for a fee, to guide them across. America put up the money and Bush's friend Tony Blair provided British Special Forces to manage the movements. People like Ehmed became richer than they had ever imagined. When the war was over, they used the money to set up contracting companies, build hotels, and create for their children a future they had never anticipated for themselves.

When it was over and Iraq had been liberated from Saddam and freed to adopt a western liberal democracy it had no interest in and no intention of making a home for, Westwood had visited Ehmed in Erbil. They had caroused together, fornicated in neighbouring brothel stalls, and sworn undying friendship. But since then, Ehmed had gone one way and Westwood another. Ehmed's way had been to build a family and a business. Westwood's had been to become a real mercenary. It never crossed Westwood's mind to start a family – or even a permanent relationship with a woman – because it would not be fair. He did not expect to live long enough to raise children, and Westwood had a number of rules he lived by. One was not leaving people in the shit by making promises, like marriage vows and vows on behalf of people being baptised who were too young to make them for themselves, that he did not expect to be there to keep.

And nor did he let people down. Even people like the Iranian spy masters he sometimes worked for. Even people like Cantrell, Annabelle and Mary Spilling. He might dislike them, he might even hold them in contempt, but once a John Buchan fan always a John Buchan fan and the word of a John Buchan follower was his bond.

But the books of John Buchan also taught other values. Betrayal could never be forgiven. It must be avenged. Dominic Carter had tried to kill Westwood, and Westwood had had to end Carter's life instead. It had been like old times and he had relished the chance to show he still had all the moves, all the street smarts, all the cunning. But it couldn't end there. Carter hadn't been the one to decide that Westwood was now disposable. Someone had sent him. Westwood didn't know who that someone was, because the people who ordered and paid for the things he did had always kept one or two cutouts between themselves and him. But he did know The Lodge, and he did know Jamaica House, and he had no doubt that Mary Spilling, chatelaine of both those establishments, knew who the paymasters were. He decided to make his way to The Lodge and shake the information out of her. If she wasn't there, he'd make for Jamaica House.

It wasn't a decision someone in full control of his mental processes would have made. But that hadn't described Westwood for some years now.

* * *

When Blazeley had given his instructions for a watch to be kept on the area in which the Range Rover had vanished, what he had hoped was to find out where it was going. That was not to be. A police surveillance team with high-level concealment skills had been deployed, but when Annabelle appeared in front of one of the surveillance cars in the

Range Rover and tucked in behind her in what he hoped was an inconspicuous way, a burst of ferocious acceleration told the cop he'd been spotted within ten seconds. He called the control room and the control room called the other cars and told them to intercept. Surrounded by police cars in front and behind, Annabelle abandoned her attempt to flee. When instructed, she stepped out of her car and into the back of one of the police cars. Since the Range Rover was suspected of possibly having been involved in illegal activity, one of the drivers waited with it until it could be taken away in a forensically secure full lift.

When they reached there, a shift change had just taken place in the custody suite and the custody sergeant who had just come on duty watched the little procession entered his domain. He said, 'I love a parade. Who is this?'

'She gave her name as Becky Smith. She was driving a Range Rover that was the subject of a watch instruction circulated by DCI Blazeley and the driver was to be arrested in connection with the murder of the man believed to be called Dominic Carter.'

'What were the circumstances of her arrest?'

'She's been arrested on suspicion of murder. In accordance with instructions received, we stopped her Range Rover. It's being brought back here for scenes of crime to look at it.'

The custody sergeant said to Annabelle, 'You have been arrested on suspicion of murder. I'm going to authorise your detention to secure and preserve evidence and obtain evidence by questioning. Do you understand?' When Annabelle simply shrugged, the sergeant went on, 'Given that we are about to take charge of everything in your pockets, I'm going to ask if your name is really Becky Smith.'

Annabelle shrugged again. 'My driving licence says I'm Annabelle Tomkins. I go by both names. Take your pick.'

'If that's the ID you have, I'll book you as Annabelle Tomkins.' He turned to a female constable and said, 'Search her, please.'

Annabelle was photographed, her height was recorded and her fingerprints were taken and checked against the database. No match appeared. When the sergeant asked whether she wanted a copy of the code of practice, she said she did. 'And I need to make a phone call.'

'That is your right. You are entitled to free and independent legal advice. We can call the duty solicitor or you can nominate one. Do you want a solicitor?'

'The person I want to call will arrange for a lawyer. And I won't talk to anyone until that lawyer is here. '

'That is your right,' said the custody sergeant again.

* * *

When Blazeley was told of the arrest of Annabelle Tomkins, he asked for scenes of crime to check over the Range Rover as soon and as thoroughly as possible. Fifteen minutes later, he was called upstairs by Detective Superintendent Chris McAvoy.

'I've just been with the chief constable,' said McAvoy. 'Annabelle Tomkins. What do you know about her?'

'As yet, almost nothing. She also uses the name Becky Smith, so I assume that she is the one who gave the story to *The Post*. She was driving a car belonging to a company called Sovereign Research who are under investigation by South Wales Police and were also the employers of Dominic Carter.'

'He's the dead guy we originally thought was Thomas Westwood?'

'That's right. But I don't know any more because she's arranging her own representation and she won't be interviewed until her lawyer arrives. What's the Chief's interest?'

'She's had a call from someone in the Home Office. Apparently, what happens to Annabelle Tomkins is a matter of interest to the kind of people who don't normally concern themselves with what goes on in a place like Batterton.'

'Are they attempting to interfere in our case?'

'I get the feeling that might have been the intention. But you know the Chief Constable. She sent them off with a flea in their ear. Told them that Tomkins would get exactly the same treatment as anyone else arrested by this force. But she did make it clear to me that we have to be able to demonstrate that everything is done by the book. No shortcuts.'

'Shortcuts. Is that something she thinks I'm known for?'

McAvoy raised a hand. 'Don't get excited, Bill. You have her complete support and you also have mine. We can't influence how the CPS deals with any evidence we put before them, and my guess would be that the Home Office can. But let's get that evidence and make it as firm and unquestionable as possible. Okay?'

'Okay. Of course.'

'Good man. Keep me in touch. And, Bill. This is not some TV dramatization. No one in some distant office is going to be allowed to pull strings. Not during our part of the operation, at any rate – we have no influence over the skulduggery that might go on afterwards. Just do your job as a policeman in the same way as you would with anyone else we'd arrested. When do you expect your guys to interview the Tomkins woman?'

'When her lawyer gets here. In the meantime, we've had the two lawyers, Patel and Mayfield, brought in. That's going to be an interesting one.'

'The way I hear it, Patel has no friends in this building.'

'She's thrown her weight around when she's had the chance. And she's insulted a number of cops individually and the police force as a whole.'

'And now she's quite probably going to be disbarred. If that happens, Bill, it happens – but make sure she's fairly treated at interview. I take it you'll have Gareth Forrester and Sally Barnes on our side of the desk?'

'I think so. They are the two best we have.'

'Remind them that everything said in that room will be recorded. And people will listen to it. They'll be looking for ways to challenge the evidence. Whatever feelings the interviewers have about the woman they must keep to themselves. We don't want anyone appealing afterwards because they can claim the interviewers showed bias.'

'Gareth and Sally are as professional as any officers I know.'

'And they have the opportunity to make this force proud of them. Make sure they know it.'

* * *

Harold Frobisher called Cantrell. 'What's the urgency?'

'Harold. You were supposed to take care of Westwood while he was in Batterton. You haven't done it, and now we have people looking into things we'd rather weren't looked into.'

'What things? Which people? Aren't you supposed to be good at suppressing investigations?'

'With a chief of police like the one you have, Harold, that isn't easy. Let's focus on damage limitation. We need to get Westwood into hiding as far from there as possible. Where is he now?'

'Where is Westwood? I haven't the faintest idea.'

'Harold. We were asked – I personally was asked – to help get you and Jensen Bartholomew out of a mess. A mess of your own making that threatened to spill over and damage your wife. I agreed because we've already had more trouble in this Parliament than we want to see and the last thing we needed was an MP of our party tainted by suggestions of illegal behaviour. Even a minor, fringe MP like Jenny Frobisher.'

Frobisher had been in the game too long to be browbeaten by someone with as weak a position as Cantrell's. He laughed. 'You agreed because you had taken a chunk of the proceeds of Bartholomew's trade with embargoed regimes. The party has nothing to do with this – I bet the chief whip knows nothing about it and the PM certainly doesn't. Whatever you've done, you've done to protect your own interests and keep yourself out of jail.'

'I asked you to monitor Westwood. Keep an eye on him. Know what he was doing, and make sure he stayed on the rails.'

'On the rails? Those must be very odd rails. Jensen Bartholomew wanted his brother Cedric killed to keep him quiet, and you went along with that. You sent a professional killer to do the job and you asked me to look after him without telling me the guy was nuts.'

'I didn't tell you because I didn't know. Westwood was once one of the best special forces operators this country ever had. And he was driven by patriotism. If those people got the recognition and honours their work deserves, Westwood would be in the House of Lords. His mental state has deteriorated, probably because of the stress he was under for so long and because, instead of rewarding him, we cut him loose on a pension that wouldn't keep a cat alive when some underworked overpaid clown in the Ministry of Defence decided we no longer needed what people like Westwood offer. A bad mistake, Harold, because we will always need what people like Westwood offer.'

'You chose the wrong guy, Cantrell. Now you want me to feel responsible and that isn't going to work. I've no idea where Westwood is and I'm not going to make it my business to find out. You sent him here – you find him and get him out.' It was with great satisfaction that Frobisher hung up the phone. His wife might take a high-handed tone and order him about, but he was damned if he'd let anyone else do it.

* * *

Meanwhile, the unwitting subject of that conversation was behind a hedge hundred yards from The Lodge, watching closely for any sign of habitation. He'd approached the area over the fields, staying as far from roads and the occasional farm building as possible. In his pocket he had the knife that had killed Ali Badaan, the gun that had killed Dominic Carter, and the Beretta that he was sure Carter had intended to use on him and had taken when he reversed the circumstances.

So far, nothing in The Lodge had moved. That was all right. When he was on a mission, Westwood could be as patient as he needed to be. And he regarded this very much as a mission.

CHAPTER 20

It was not in Adina Patel's nature to submit to interrogation without taking the fight to the interviewer. She said, 'Why am I here? Of what offence am I accused?'

The two specialist interviewers were prepared for this approach. Sally Barnes said, 'You are under arrest on suspicion of blackmailing Cedric Bartholomew. When you were brought to the station, the custody sergeant will have repeated that information. Did you fail to hear what they said?'

Adina's gesture could have indicated anything. Sally said, 'You have been offered legal representation. It is my understanding that you have decided that you don't need to be represented by a lawyer, but will you please confirm that decision for the tape?'

'I am a lawyer and I can represent myself without outside assistance.'

'Will you also please confirm that you have been told that you can change your mind at any time and that if you do so the interview will be suspended until a lawyer is here and you have had an opportunity to talk to them in private?'

The lawyer rolled her eyes. 'Yes, yes, I am happy to confirm that. Can we please get on with this?'

'Did you, in fact, blackmail Cedric Bartholomew?'

Adina had not known until this moment how she was going to respond to that question. She had considered a simple "No comment," but in the cold light of day with the question out there in the open she realised how pointless that would be. The reason police use specialist interviewers since the introduction of PACE is to manoeuvre suspects into either saying something that will later be presented in court as evidence against them or into not saying something that, because they did not raise it at the time, would be difficult for them to use in a trial. If she answered no comment to all the questions she was asked, the interviewers would make sure that her silence made it very easy for a jury to bring in a guilty verdict. And she was guilty. So what was the point? She was likely to lose everything she'd worked so hard to establish – but she had blackmailed Cedric Bartholomew. She'd done it to raise money for causes she regarded as impeccable – but blackmail is against the law and she had blackmailed Cedric Bartholomew. She might just as well get it all over with now. 'Yes,' she said. 'I blackmailed Cedric Bartholomew.'

'What did you have against him that made it worth his while to pay you?'

'He and his brother, Jensen Bartholomew, had conspired to sell high-technology goods to countries to which their sale was embargoed. I had evidence to that effect. The evidence was in three files that were stored in our office, protected by the most advanced security devices. Those files were stolen. They were passed to a journalist and it's my understanding that they are now in your possession.'

Gareth Forrester said, 'You say that the files implicated Jensen Bartholomew as well as Cedric Bartholomew?'

'You have the files.'

'Ms Patel, did the files implicate Jensen Bartholomew as well as Cedric Bartholomew?'

'Yes, they did. They do.'

'Then why did you not blackmail Jensen Bartholomew as well as his brother?'

'I did invite Jensen Bartholomew also to contribute to our work. Because that's what it was – you call it blackmail, but I would describe it as collecting contributions to valuable work for the protection of vulnerable people who, without our help, were liable to be deported to countries where their lives would be in danger.'

'You attempted to blackmail Jensen Bartholomew as well as his brother.'

'If you insist on using that word, then yes, I did.'

'And what was his response?'

'He laughed at me. He said some things I'm not prepared to repeat. Things that were both racist and sexist. He also said… Well, never mind that.'

Sally said, 'What was it he also said?'

Adina stared at them both without speaking.

Gareth said, 'You keep using the word "I." I blackmailed Cedric Bartholomew. I invited Jansen Bartholomew to contribute. But it wasn't just you, was it? Christina Mayfield was also…'

'Christina knew nothing about it. She was not involved at any point. I was the only person committing what you think of as an offence.'

'Well, we shall see Ms Mayfield has to say about that. We are going to leave you here for a few minutes while we talk to senior officers. They will decide what the next steps are going to be. But my advice would be that you should not expect to go home tonight. The custody sergeant will ask you later whether there is anything you would like us to do to make it easier for you to stay here.'

'Easy!'

'A change of clothes, perhaps. A word to anyone who might be waiting for you. Looking after a pet…'

'No one is waiting for me and I don't have any pets.'

'Well, you may change your mind by the time the custody sergeant speaks to you. In the meantime, we're going to move you back to the cells. You should know that you will be monitored constantly.'

'Constable, if you're afraid that I may seek to avoid the grubby business you are engaged in by ending my own life, you don't know me.'

When they were outside the room, Gareth said to Sally, 'Don't know her? I'm glad not to know her. What a self-righteous person she is.'

Sally said, 'I wonder what it was she started to say and then stopped herself?'

'I've no idea. But perhaps we'll find out when we interview the other one. '

* * *

And they did. They went through with Christina Mayfield the same initial steps that they had been through with Adina Patel, and she told them very much the same things. Then, when she had confirmed that both Bartholomew brothers had been engaged in illegal work, Sally said, 'Was anyone else involved?'

'Yes. Harold Frobisher. Husband of Jenny Frobisher MP.'

'Say some more about that.'

'Flogging stuff to countries that aren't supposed to have it isn't simple. You need documentation and some of it has to be authenticated. The authentication will be illegal. Obviously. Someone is putting a stamp on an invoice or certificate of origin or bill of lading to say that the goods being shipped are goods that that country is not banned from receiving, when that isn't true. Harold Frobisher has contacts prepared and able to apply that stamp. For a fee. But you have the files that was stolen from our office – you must know that.'

'There is nothing in the files about Jensen Bartholomew or Harold Frobisher.'

Christina sat in silence for a while. At last she said, 'Then the files have been doctored. You need to look at whoever gave them to you.'

Gareth said, 'These files must have been confidential. I mean, to the previous owners. So how did they come into your possession?'

'No comment.'

'Did you steal them?'

'I've never stolen anything in my life.'

'Did Adina Patel steal them?'

'I'm sure Adina would give you the same answer as I just did.'

Sally said, 'Ms Mayfield, we are now going to terminate this interview and talk to senior officers. You will be returned to the cells. Our senior officers will tell us what they want us to do, but you have admitted the serious offence of blackmail and I shall be very surprised if they don't tell us to approach the CPS for authority to charge you and hold you overnight until we can put you in front of a magistrate. The custody sergeant will come in at some point to ask who should be informed that you are being held, and what assistance you might need.'

'My cats will need to be fed.'

'Cats?'

'I have three.'

'The custody sergeant will get the details from you. Your cats will not be allowed to go hungry.'

'And someone needs to tell our receptionist to close the office. We both have immigration hearings at which we are due to speak on behalf of our clients. I don't suppose…'

Sally said, 'Your office is already closed, Ms Mayfield. There will be a crime scene tape across the door. So your receptionist will know. Scenes of crime officers are looking for evidence. And if you were going to ask whether you could be released to attend hearings, I'm afraid that won't be possible.'

'No. The Law Society…'

'We haven't advised them directly, but we have issued a press release. It's very unlikely that no journalist will have asked them to comment. So, if that's what you were going to ask, I think you can assume that the Law Society knows you have both been arrested. And tomorrow, if the CPS gives us the instructions we expect them to give, they will know that you have both been charged. '

Christina looked at the floor. 'It's all over, then. My career, I mean.' She made a weak attempt at a smile, but it wouldn't have taken anyone in. 'I'd better learn to ask whether people want fries with their burger.'

* * *

When Gareth and Sally went to the room where Susanna and Blazeley had been monitoring the interviews, Blazeley congratulated them both. 'Well done, both of you. An excellent job. There are some things we still don't know – like how they came to have the files and whether information implicating Jensen Bartholomew and Harold Frobisher really has been removed – but we can still move things forward. I'll speak to the CPS and get their agreement to charge the pair of them. And it seems to me the accusation against Jensen Bartholomew will be enough to arrest him on suspicion. Which means we can put SOCO into his house and his office to see what turns up.

Susanna said, 'And Harold Frobisher?'

'I think we'd better hold off on that. Searching his house means searching his wife's house, and his wife is an MP.

Let's see if what we find at Bartholomew's place strengthens suspicion against Frobisher.

CHAPTER 21

Chris McAvoy eyed Blazeley with caution. 'You've arrested Jensen Bartholomew? Bloody hell, Bill. We're going to look pretty sick if we don't turn anything up. And Bartholomew is not without powerful friends. We've already had people trying to interfere in this case. Haven't you got anything more than the word of a solicitor whose about to be struck off?'

Blazeley had brought Susanna David with him, and she said, 'What about Maisie?'

'Maisie?' said McAvoy.

'Maisie Bertrand from forensic accountancy,' said Blazeley. 'She thinks Bartholomew has been hiding things in his books. We assumed it was some kind of tax fiddle. But if what he's hiding is illegal shipments…'

McAvoy said, 'It's your call, Bill. You're the SIO. Let's hope Maisie finds something.'

* * *

There was just time to ring Maisie and get her confirmation that she wasn't going to say Bartholomew was definitely hiding information about illegal shipments but nor was she going to say he definitely wasn't before the custody sergeant rang to say that Annabelle Tomkins's lawyer had arrived. 'And a more toffee-nosed, patronising git it has never been my misfortune to meet.'

Blazeley said, 'I imagine he'll want to spend time with his client before we can interview her.'

'Not a bit of it. He was in with her for two minutes. Now he says he wants her dealt with so that she can be given bail and he can take her out of here. I gather he's brought a prepared statement with him. All she has to do is sign it and keep her mouth shut.'

'We'll see about that. I've just got to arrange some more business for you and then I'll instruct Sally and Gareth to get on with it.'

'You're arresting someone else?'

'Jensen Bartholomew.'

'Good grief.'

* * *

When he had told Rayyan and Theresa to arrest Jensen Bartholomew, Blazeley went with Susanna to brief Gareth

245

and Sally about interviewing Annabelle Tomkins. 'What we really want to know is where she was taking that car and on whose instructions. Remember, it's registered to Sovereign Research. We'd like to know as much as we can about them, her connection with them, and how she came to be in a vehicle belonging to them. She isn't going to want to say anything, and her lawyer is going to give her all possible assistance in that. The advantage we have is that they think we are a bunch of yokels who don't need to be taken seriously. Show them they are wrong. They will want to threaten you with intervention from people more powerful than us. If you can demonstrate amusement in response to that, you just might get a rise out of them and someone may say something they don't want to say. But I think you'll find that the lawyer will say as little as he can get away with and he will have told Annabelle not to say anything at all. Before you go in there, reread the article in *The Post* where she pretended to be Becky Smith. And take the paper in with you. The lawyer is going to demand bail. You can tell him that your instructions are that no bail can be granted until we have a clear understanding of why she told Bernadette Spence that Westwood had had someone fed to pigs at Jamaica House. See what she says to that. Press her on her relationship with Westwood. Also, take the pictures from the meeting with Bernadette Spence at Parkway Station. Good luck. Susanna and I will be watching.'

The lawyer began as soon as they got into the room. 'At last! Do you know how long we've been kept waiting? I want my client bailed right now.'

Gareth and Sally ignored the outburst. Gareth set up the recording equipment and spoke to give the place, date and time, and his name. Then Sally said, 'DC Sally Barnes.'

The lawyer said, 'Is this a joke? Two detective constables? Is no one more senior available?'

Sally said, 'Could you give your name for the recording, please? So that the transcriber will be able to identify you?'

The lawyer tutted his irritation. 'Jolyon Matravers.'

Sally looked towards Annabelle, who said, 'Annabelle Tomkins.'

'Thank you,' said Sally. She gave Annabelle a formal caution. Then the lawyer said, 'I have here a statement which I shall read on behalf of Ms Tomkins. The statement says everything that Ms Tomkins has any intention of communicating. She will answer no questions after the statement has been read.' He opened a leather folder marked with the initials JM and took out a single A4 sheet, from which he read, 'My name is Annabelle Tomkins. I was driving a Range Rover that I had been told needed to be returned to a car rental company in Batterton. I agreed to return it as a favour because it was explained to me that the person who had hired it had become ill and was unable to return it herself. I did not ask and do not

247

know the name of that person or of the person who asked me to return the car. I was driving, lawfully and within the speed limit, when I was suddenly chased by another car. If I had known it was a police car, I would of course have stopped, but I did not, and so I feared an attack and I attempted to escape. When I was stopped by other cars, I realised that I was dealing with the police and I immediately ceased trying to get away. I have no idea why I am here.' The lawyer put the statement on the desk and passed it to the two officers. 'You will see that this statement is signed by Ms Tomkins and witnessed by me. That is all the information my client has. I now propose to leave here and take her with me.'

He stood up and reached out an arm towards Annabel. She stood and turned towards the door.

Gareth said, 'Ms Tomkins. You are under arrest and you have been cautioned. We will be the ones to decide when you leave here. And I'm afraid that that time has not come. Please sit down.'

When Matravers sat, Annabelle followed his example. The lawyer said, 'We are remaining here under protest. As I have already told you, my client will answer no questions.'

Gareth said, 'Ms Tomkins. Who owns the car you were driving when you were arrested?'

A glance flashed between Annabelle and her lawyer, before Annabelle said, 'No comment.'

Gareth said, 'You suggested that you were to return it to a rental company but, in fact, the car is registered to Sovereign Research. Do you have any connection with Sovereign Research?'

'No comment.'

'Had you ever seen that car before you say you were asked to return it to a rental company?'

'No comment.'

'Do you know a man called Thomas Westwood?'

'No comment.'

Sally placed the newspaper on the table open at the page with the story that contained the little that the editor and Susanna David between them had been prepared to allow her to publish. 'Ms Tomkins. Do you remember speaking about Thomas Westwood to Bernadette Spence, a reporter at *The Post*?'

'No comment.'

'Did you tell Bernadette Spence your name was Becky Smith?

'No comment.'

'Did you tell Bernadette Spence that a body had been eaten by pigs in the gardens of Jamaica House?'

'No comment.'

Gareth placed a photograph face up on the table. 'Is this you, Ms Tomkins?'

'No comment.'

Gareth, 'For the tape, I have just shown Ms Tomkins the photograph identified as JH/1.' He placed another photograph on the table. 'I am now showing Ms Tomkins the photograph identified as JH/2. Ms Tomkins, will you please tell me who this is?'

Shock was obvious on Annabelle's face, but after a pause she said, 'No comment.'

'This is the photograph identified as JH/3. It shows a car. The car is driven by the man in photograph JH/2 and carries as a passenger the woman in photograph JH/1. Ms Tomkins, will you please confirm that you are passenger in this car?'

'No comment.'

'And will you confirm that the car in photograph JH/3 is the Range Rover that you were driving when you were arrested and brought here?'

'No comment.'

'How can you possibly expect a jury to believe that that car was given to you by a complete stranger with the request that you return it to a rental company when you had been photographed in it some days earlier?'

'No comment.'

'What can you tell us about the death of a man called Dominic Carter?'

'No comment.'

'Ms Tomkins, you will now be taken back to your cell. We are going to speak to our senior officers to recommend we approach CPS for authority to charge you with Dominic Carter's murder. If the CPS agree, your lawyer will confirm to you there can be no question of bail being granted in the case of a murder charge. A magistrate does not have the power to grant bail in cases of murder. You will therefore be held here overnight.'

Matravers said, 'I want time to speak to my client.'

'Of course,' said Sally. 'You can have all the time you want. But I feel I should tell you that we have already been instructed by senior officers that there will be no movement in our position today unless your client is prepared to name the person in the photograph identified as JH/2 and to be entirely open with us about her relationship with the man known as Thomas Westwood.' She dictated the time at which the interview was being suspended and stopped the recording.

CHAPTER 22

Jensen Bartholomew's face was the picture of fury as he was taken to a cell by the custody sergeant. Bernadette Spence, on the other hand, showed something approaching joy when she looked at the stream of press releases coming out of Batterton police station. They were giving her not just a story for *The Post* but also one she could offer to the national newspapers where she still hoped to spend the next stage of her career. But *The Post* had to come first. The editor raised his eyebrows at the draft she submitted but said nothing. What appeared in the paper was somewhat shorter than Bernie's draft and read as follows:

Arrests in Murder Cases

Batterton police have been carrying out a series of arrests in connection with investigations into the murders of Cedric Bartholomew, Yuri Malinov, Ali Badaan and Dominic Carter. Del Theobald, as readers will be aware, is already on remand charged with the murders of Malinov and Badaan.

First among those additionally arrested were lawyers Adina Patel and Christina Mayfield. This was followed by the arrest of Jensen Bartholomew, brother of the late Cedric Bartholomew.

We will bring you further developments as they occur.

Bernie was sufficiently irritated by the cuts to her story to decide to put into place Plan B, which she had been contemplating since the reaction to her earlier story – a reaction that had now seen the deputy editor released in disgrace by *The Post.* The B in Plan B stood for Blog. Bernie had already set up a blog entitled *Crime Uncovered* with a company in Kazakhstan. She had used a VPN to pretend that she was in Colombia and had used that to establish a Facebook page and a Twitter account with the same name. No one who knew Bernie Spence would have any doubt that the blog's long-term purpose was to build her reputation to the point where the national press would finally understand her true value and where books bearing her name as author would find a ready market. For now, though, she understood the necessity of not being identified as the blog's author. People could suspect anything they liked and no doubt they would – but suspecting something and proving it are two different things, as the CPS had just pointed out to Bill Blazeley and Susanna David in respect of Annabelle Tomkins. The blog now carried the following post, which was remarkably close to the version that she had seen mercilessly slashed by *The Post*'s editor:

Arrests Indicate Breakthrough by Police

Crime Uncovered Special Reporter

In the UK, Batterton police have been carrying out a series of arrests that suggest an imminent breakthrough in investigations into the murders of Cedric Bartholomew, Yuri Malinov, Ali Badaan and Dominic Carter. Del Theobald is already on remand charged with the murders of Malinov and Badaan, but Theobald was a known denizen of the town's criminal fraternity. The most recent arrests involve people from a less likely social stratum.

First among those arrested were prominent immigration lawyers and activists Adina Patel and Christina Mayfield. It was already common knowledge and had indeed been published in the local newspaper, The Post, that these ladies had been guilty of serious criminal offences that may have led, directly or indirectly, to the death of Cedric Bartholomew. The Law Society has confirmed that their status as qualified practitioners is suspended and they are not permitted to practice until they have answered to the charges in court.

Their arrest was followed by that of a woman charged under the name of Annabelle Tomkins, who has previously presented newspapers with very dubious stories while calling herself Becky Smith. In this case, and for reasons we find incomprehensible, we understand that the Crown Prosecution Service has refused Batterton police authority to charge Ms Tomkins (if that really is her name) with any offence.

All of this would already have astounded the law-abiding people of the town of Batterton, but an even more astonishing piece of information emerged today when it was announced that another man has been arrested charged with involvement in the unlawful killing of Cedric Bartholomew – in this case, the victim's only brother, Jensen Bartholomew.

This reporter is keeping a close eye on the doings of Batterton police and will bring you further developments as they occur. Meanwhile, it will interest readers to know that Batterton's member of Parliament, Jenny Frobisher, is believed to be not without involvement in these sordid goings-on. There has even been some suggestion that illegal trade with embargoed nations may be at the root of the matter.

When Jensen Bartholomew had escorted her off the premises, he'd made what any normal person would have seen as a threat to her personal safety. But if you'd said that to Bernie, she'd have said, 'Normal? Who wants to be normal?' And, in any case, how much harm could Bartholomew do her now? That he might already have asked someone to deal with her didn't cross her mind and when her phone rang she did not hear the warning bells that might have been audible to a more cautious person. She should have been more alert. A post on a new blog would normally attract no one's attention, but that was not true of the tweet that accompanied it and went viral.

Bernie's caller was a woman, and she sounded a little frightened. 'You want the lowdown on why Cedric Bartholomew had to die? I've got the whole story. I'm sorry, I can't tell you on the phone. I've suspected for a while that my phone is tapped.'

If ever there were words designed to attract Bernie, they were, "My phone is tapped." If anyone would go to the trouble of tapping someone's phone, the someone must have something worth hearing. Mustn't they? 'Where are you? Who are you?'

'Who I am you'll find out when you get here. Where I am… Do you have a satnav?'

'I have an iPhone.'

'Good. Write down this postcode. How soon can you get here?'

'I've no idea. I don't recognise the postcode and I won't know where it is until I'm in my car. But I'm going to set off right now.'

'Good. Please don't leave that postcode anywhere someone might see it, and don't tell anyone you're coming here. I'm in too much danger already.'

That the meeting was worthwhile was reinforced even more strongly. Bernie thought of saying she would chew the postcode and swallow it, but the woman sounded too frightened to be amused by a joke. Bernie left a note on her desk to say that she was on a call, keyed the postcode into her phone, went down to the car

park underneath the building, and set off.

* * *

At The Lodge, Mary Spilling who had made the call, put down the phone. Cantrell said, 'You think she bought it?'

'She's a journalist. She isn't going to pass up an opportunity like that.'

'I hope you're right. I believe she is also a secret blogger, and I can't let her continue. I came here because of a panic call from Jensen Bartholomew. You know him?'

She shook her head. 'I've heard the name, of course. I never met him.'

'I've often had cause to wish I hadn't. But he's in trouble, the overflow might affect me and I can't let that happen so here I am. The day might not end well for Ms Spence. If you decide you'd rather not be here, I'll understand.'

'I think I'll take you up on that.'

'That's probably the sensible thing to do. And go somewhere people will see you and be able to give you an alibi. Just in case.'

She walked out of the house, got into her car and was about to drive off when she felt a slight movement behind her. 'Who's there?'

A knife pressed against her throat. 'Hello, Mary. It's been a while.'

'Westwood? What do you want? And take that knife away.'

'Perhaps not right this minute, Mary. Drive the car out of the driveway. Turn left. I'll tell you when to stop. And then we'll have a little chat.'

* * *

In the room he and Annabelle Tomkins had been taken to after her interview, Jolyon Matravers said, 'Well done, Annabelle. All you need do now is carry on saying nothing. These people,' and he gestured towards the door, 'have nothing on you. Even if they persuade a local magistrate to remand you in custody, it will be a few days at most. If you find your fellows there unspeakable, ask to be placed in solitary confinement. You were driving a car that had previously been driven by someone of interest to the police.

Whatever they say, they can't connect the car with any murder. You told a highly embroidered story to a journalist in return for money. That's not a crime. I shall be making representations to the Crown Court and the very least I can promise is that you will be remanded on bail in a very short space of time. You will probably have to surrender your passport for the time being but you will be free to do whatever you like in this country. Can you manage a few days of boring company and execrable food?'

'I was at boarding school for six years.'

'Quite so. I shall leave you now; I'll make it clear to the custody sergeant that any attempt to talk to you without me there will be met with a very firm reaction. But don't worry – these people are accustomed to people very different from you and they know that.' He stood. 'I'll go now. Any message for your parents?'

She shook her head. 'Just tell them what's happening.'

'Your mother thinks you should never have got involved with Cantrell.'

'I know. But my mother has no excitement in her life. And no desire for it.'

* * *

Hannah Brian had told Rayann and Nicola about The Lodge, and they had had a uniformed PC drive through Pinkline once or twice and keep an eye on the place through binoculars. He had reported back that there was no sign of movement and the place seemed empty.

Today, however, he had driven past on other business and phoned in to say that he had seen lights in one of the rooms. Control had passed that information to Susanna David and she had rounded up Rayann and Nicola and asked them to check it out. 'I can't go with you because we have all these interviews going on and I need to watch them.'

When they were in the car, Nicola said, 'She isn't supposed to be out in the field anyway. Inspectors are supposed to be managers. They pull all the threads together, but it's us constables and sergeants who actually get out and do stuff.'

'She's never really given up on that part of the job, though. I think she finds management a bit boring.'

* * *

And that was probably true. But Susanna wasn't bored by what she was doing now, which was watching Jensen Bartholomew being interviewed.

Bartholomew had not needed to accept the custody sergeant's offer of a duty solicitor. After Bernie Spence had visited him to ask questions about his possible involvement in his brother's death and in the illegal sale of goods to Iran, his call to Cantrell had begun the chain of events that now had the unsuspecting Bernie driving on what Cantrell intended to be the last journey she would make until she travelled in a hearse. But that was not the only purpose of the call. Bartholomew had also asked for the name of a competent lawyer. When he went into the interview room with Gareth Forester and Sally Barnes, he was accompanied by Helena Booth. Helena had been to Batterton only once before – a few days ago, when she came to rehearse Bartholomew in the way he must behave if arrested and interviewed – but her reputation was well known. Blazeley said to the two interviewers, 'There's nothing crafty about this one. She won't try to trip you up. She'll treat you with respect. But don't be fooled. Bartholomew will be paying her top dollar. And she's worth it. Out of every ten people this woman represents, five never reach court and only one of the five who do is convicted. The case isn't over when we arrest someone – that's when it starts. Helena Booth knows that as well as we do and she will guide Bartholomew to the answers that mean the CPS will decide we don't have a prosecutable case.'

They went through the process of setting up the recording equipment and introducing themselves for the convenience of the transcriber. Then Sally repeated the caution Bartholomew had already received. 'I want to ask you some questions.'

Bartholomew gave her an excellent impression of a friendly smile. 'Please do. It's obvious there's been some dreadful misunderstanding. The sooner we put it to bed and I can go home, the better. I'll help all I can.'

It took all Sally's concentration to prevent a smile crossing her face. This was so far from the bluster, the pointless demands, the insults and the shouting that started most interviews. She said, 'Have you ever been involved in the sale of goods to countries embargoed – by this country or any other – from receiving those goods?'

'Certainly not. My father built this business and he built it on honesty and integrity. He would turn in his grave at the very thought I would do such a thing.'

'And yet,' said Gareth, 'evidence exists that your brother Cedric has done just that.'

Bartholomew's face was so like a drama school student's *Sadness Exercise 1* that Gareth felt like applauding. Bartholomew said, 'I cannot tell you how appalled I was when I learned that. But I knew nothing of it at the time. And I'm still not convinced it's true.'

Sally said, 'Have you ever been to Iran?'

'Not for a number of years.'

'But you do know the country? Do you still have contacts there?'

Bartholomew stepped up a gear to *Sadness Exercise 2*. 'I had some dear friends there. People I was proud to do business with. But there has been no word from any of them for some years, and I fear…' For a moment, Gareth thought he was actually going to squeeze out a tear. 'Do you know that under its present government Iran executes more people than any country except China? If they stick to what Amnesty International says is their daily average, three people will be hanged there today. They will have hanged three yesterday and they'll hang another three tomorrow.' He shook his head. 'They hang them in public from high cranes, because the purpose is not to punish wrongdoers – it's to keep the population in a state of abject terror.' He leaned forward a little. 'And you want to know if I do business with people like that?'

It was a bravura performance. Nevertheless, it was necessary to keep this interview going because they had to give SOCO time to go through Bartholomew's house and office. Sally said, 'We know about your brother's involvement because of three files that have come into our possession.'

Helena Booth said, 'And that is why my client is not convinced of his brother's guilt. I'm going to need details of the provenance of those files. I shall be asking to see the chain of evidence.'

'Of course,' said Sally, though her heart sank at the thought of what lawyers of this quality could do with those details. The files had been held by two lawyers who were now in process of being struck off and would shortly face trial for using what was in the files to blackmail Cedric Bartholomew. They had been stolen and the only evidence the police had suggested that the thief had been Cedric Bartholomew, but he was now dead and could not be questioned. The police had no idea where the files had gone after that until they were handed to a reporter by a woman who might be called Annabelle Tomkins, though she might also be called Becky Smith. The journalist had held them for a while before giving them to the police. There were so many holes in the chain of evidence that the CPS would never sanction a prosecution based on the files alone. Of course, they also had Patel and Mayfield's confessions, but how much weight would a jury place on the word of disgraced lawyers? Especially when the sort of QC that a woman like Helena Booth would be likely to instruct attacked it?

* * *

Similar thoughts were being expressed in the room where Bill Blazeley and Susanna David were watching the interview on monitors. Blazeley said, 'When the lawyer arrived, she only spent two minutes with Bartholomew and yet he's performing impeccably. What do we deduce?'

'That wasn't the first time they met. She's already rehearsed him.'

'Which means?'

'He suspected we'd come for him.'

'Exactly... And?'

'If she prepared him for an interview, she will also have warned him that we'd be turning his home and his office over.'

'That's exactly how I see it. Which means...'

'We're wasting our time. SOCO aren't going to find anything. So what do you want to do? Pull the plug?'

'It's a bit early for that. Send Sally a message. Tell her to wind it up for now, and put Bartholomew back in his cell. And call the two crime scene managers. Tell them to focus on the unlikely – anything obvious will be gone. And say we'll probably release Bartholomew in a few hours. Let him get home for his tea.'

'Grilled tuna.'

'What?'

'That's his thing. Grilled tuna. He built a whole house round his passion for it.'

CHAPTER 23

When Westwood told her to, Mary Spilling drove the car into the space in front of a gate and stopped. Westwood showed her the Biretta he'd taken from Dominic Carter. 'This was supposed to be used to kill me, Mary. And I won't have any hesitation about using it to kill you. Understand that and everything will be fine. Get into the passenger seat.'

When Mary had obeyed his instructions, he moved forward into the driver's seat. The Biretta was pointing at Mary's stomach. 'So,' he said. 'The Lodge. What's happening in there?'

Mary weighed the likelihood that she would still be alive at the end of this day. If she cooperated with Westwood, told him everything she knew and did whatever he told her to do, she thought her chances of survival were poor. If she didn't, she thought they were zero. A poor chance was better than none. She said, 'Cantrell is in there.'

'And he is… Who?'

'Depends who you talk to. People use him as a fixer. If there's something you want done without publicity, and you have the money, you call Cantrell. But he also works for himself. He owns a company called Sovereign Research. Sovereign Research is the owner of The Lodge and Jamaica House.'

Westwood was staring at her in a way she didn't like. 'That's who you work for?'

'You, too. I'm on the permanent staff and you are freelance. Cantrell hired you to kill Cedric Bartholomew and pretend to threaten his brother.'

'Go on.'

'You did that. Then Cantrell decided you were a loose cannon. He sent Dominic Carter to kill you.'

'I don't get it. I never met Cantrell. Until two minutes ago I hadn't heard of him. Why kill me?'

'Cantrell likes things tidy. People doing what they are paid to do and not doing what they're not. You killed Ali Badaan, which you hadn't been hired to do. To Cantrell, that looks like a joyride. What don't you get?'

'Okay. So Cantrell is in The Lodge. Why? Is he planning to come after me himself?'

Mary shook her head. 'I wish you'd point that gun somewhere else. You're scaring me.'

'Good. Answer the question.'

'It's nothing to do with you. He's here to meet a journalist called Bernadette Spence.'

'He's going to tell her a story?'

'He's going to fix it so she never writes another story in her life. He's going to take her life away from her. She's threatening to publish a story about Jensen Bartholomew. Jensen Bartholomew is one of Cantrell's clients. He asked for help and Cantrell is giving it. That's how it works. It's how you got involved in the first place. Jensen Bartholomew told Cantrell his brother had information that could sink Bartholomew. Bartholomew could take Cantrell with him. So Cantrell told whoever it is he tells, and that person told someone else, and the someone else instructed you to kill Cedric.'

Westwood nodded. He was used to not knowing who was behind the stuff he did and it didn't trouble him, but this story made sense.

'The journalist. Is she there now?'

'Not yet. He's waiting for her.'

'She's coming from Batterton?'

'Yes.'

'So she'll pass this way. Do you know what she looks like?'

'I've seen her photograph in the paper.'

'Then we'll sit here and wait till she goes past. Make yourself comfortable.'

'That would be easier without a gun pointing at me.'

'Possibly. But do your best anyway.'

* * *

The initial word from the crime scene managers at both Jensen Bartholomew locations was not positive. If there was anything here, they didn't recognise it. What they did recognise were signs that someone had beaten them to it. The side had been removed from a bath in one of Bartholomew's bathrooms. The office safe had been emptied. It was clear that the back had been removed from a Picasso print and then replaced. 'Something was hidden behind it,' said Bazeley. 'We are wasting our time.'

Susanna said, 'I hate it when we know someone is guilty and they get away.'

'You should be used to it by now. Sometimes we get our man and sometimes we don't. There's no point letting it upset you.'

'So what are we going to do? Let him go?'

'I don't see that we have any choice. Smile and make the most of it.'

* * *

Mary Spilling endured ten painful minutes. She realised that the chances of Westwood letting her live were poor. Poor enough, probably, not to exist. Mary hadn't talked to God since childhood and she hadn't really believed in him even then. She didn't now. But, when you thought your life might be about to end, your mind went to places long abandoned. Then she recognised the woman driving past her. 'That's her.'

'Good.' Westwood stepped out of the car and Mary wondered if he was going to tell her to drive because he couldn't drive and at the same time hold a gun on her. Really, though, she knew she was fooling herself. It felt as though her whole life had been heading towards this ending. As Westwood was walking round to her side, she thought about jumping into the driver's seat, but who was she kidding? He opened the door and motioned her out. She said, 'Can I have a moment to pray?'

'Of course.'

She clasped her hands in front of her. 'Lord God, I'm sorry for all the things I've done that I shouldn't have done. Please forgive me.' She looked up at Westwood but saw no sympathy in his eyes. He said, 'I can't use the gun. You never know who's close enough to hear it. You might want to close your eyes.'

She did, and so she didn't see the flash of an extended knife that had been the last thing Ali Badaan saw. She sank into the grass by the gate, as dead as he had been, and Westwood got into the car, turned it around and drove back towards The Lodge.

* * *

If Westwood had waited another three minutes, he would have seen Rayyan and Nicola drive past going in the same direction as Bernie Spence had been. They had been too far behind Bernadette, but they were close enough on Westwood's heels to see him turn through the gates. Rayyann said, 'Get the number. Drive straight past. Then stop.'

A call very quickly brought back the information that the registered owner of the car they had just seen was registered to a Mary Spilling. 'The housekeeper at Jamaica House,' said Rayyann. 'But that was a man driving.' They got out of the car and walked back towards the gate through which Westwood had driven. A quick look round the corner told them that the car was parked just inside at the beginning of the driveway – but there was no one in it. Rayyann said, 'Contact the DI on your Airwave radio. Tell her Mary Spilling's car is here, there are lights on and we're going to investigate.'

* * *

If Bernadette had known that the police were here when she arrived, would she have gone ahead and entered The Lodge? When she asked herself that question later, she thought the answer was probably yes because Bernie Spence in pursuit of a story was not easily put off. She'd have been surprised, though, because whoever had called her had seemed determined on secrecy. In any case, it didn't arise because, when Bernie parked right in front of the house and walked through the front door, Rayyan and Nicola were scouting round the back. She didn't see them and they didn't see her. Westwood had seen all three of them, but The Lodge was old, it had a number of little niches and corners where someone could hide, Westwood was familiar with all of them and he was biding his time waiting to see what was going to happen.

Bernadette heard a voice saying, 'Ms Spence? In here. The front room.' It was a man's voice and Bernie had been expecting a woman but a story was a story and into the front room she went. What she saw was a man waving her towards a chair. The waving was particularly forceful because the hand doing it held a gun. She sat down. Cantrell said, 'You are a damned nuisance. You've caused me a great deal of trouble. The trouble ends now.' And he raised the gun and pointed it at her head.

Rayyan and Nicola, having entered through the back door, were by now just outside. Rayyan whispered, 'Stay here. Call for armed backup.' Then he walked into the front room and held up his warrant card. 'Detective Sergeant Padgett. Put the gun down, sir.'

Cantrell's face was a picture of astonishment. He said, 'I can't believe this. What kind of imbecile are you? Is this how the police behave in the arse end of nowhere? Don't you know you're not supposed to put yourself at risk?' He moved his head in Bernadette's direction. 'She's already signed her own death warrant. You think it will trouble me to end your paltry life, too?'

Rayyan was still moving in his direction. 'The gun, sir. Give it to me.'

'Oh, I'll give it to you all right. Between the eyes, damn you.' And he raised the gun and pulled the trigger.

Bernadette screamed. Later, she'd ask herself why and the answer would be that she thought it was probably expected of her. What she was thinking was that this was going to be the best story she'd ever filed – and all she had to do was stay alive long enough to type it. And then things happened in quick succession. They began when Westwood left his hiding place, raced into the front room and hurled himself at Cantrell. Cantrell knew exactly who his assailant was and he also knew that only one person ever emerged alive from a contretemps with Westwood. Even falling backwards with Westwood's arms round him, he retained the presence of mind to put his gun behind Westwood's ear and pull the trigger for the second time in a minute. Bernadette decided she had enough to write her story and ran. By the time Cantrell had shrugged off the weight of Westwood's body, the reporter was out of the front door and legging it towards her car. Cantrell stood at the front door, lifted the gun in both hands and steadied himself for the shot, at which point, Nicola executed one of the manoeuvres that had had her coaches prophesying Olympic gold if she would only give up the idea of a career and concentrate on the mat. By the time she had Cantrell safety cuffed, called for an ambulance and was cradling Rayyan's head in her lap, Bernadette had rung her editor, screamed, 'DON'T LET THE FRONT PAGE GO,' and was breaking every speed limit on her way back to the office.

The ambulance crew had to use something almost approaching force to prise Nicola away from Rayyan. She kept saying, 'He's alive. He's alive.'

One of the paramedics held her hand for a moment. 'We'll do our best for him, love.' But when they had Rayann in the ambulance and Nicola was watching the armed officers who had answered her call for backup taking Cantrell from the building, the paramedic said to her partner, 'He needs a miracle.'

Nicola didn't hear that. Nor did she wait for the uniformed officers who would arrive to take Cantrell to the police station. Armed officers couldn't do that, because of the risk that gunshot residue would be transferred to the arrested person's clothing while in the car, allowing defence counsel to cast doubt on the accused having fired a gun. Overcome by grief, Nicola got into her car and followed the ambulance.

CHAPTER 24

The story that appeared in *The Post* told readers that a police officer had been shot and was fighting for his life in Batterton General Hospital. It told readers that their crime reporter had actually been present and promised a full account when the trial of the people involved was over. Until then, it said, readers would understand that *The Post* could not so betray the interests of justice as to provide any information that would later be given in court.

The *Crime Uncovered* blog was somewhat more forthcoming.

BLOODY MURDER IN BATTERTON

Crime Uncovered Special Reporter

Today a young detective sergeant is fighting for his life in Batterton General Hospital — put there by a man now under arrest who had lured a reporter to a remote house intending that she should be the one to die.

Readers are probably still reeling from the information we reported yesterday that the latest person to be arrested by the police in connection with the murder of Cedric Bartholomew was the dead man's own brother, Jensen Bartholomew. How, you may think, could anyone possibly be implicated in his own brother's death?

A reporter (she has no connection with this blog and we heard this information to a third party) received a call inviting her to a remote house a few miles from Batterton. The caller — a woman — said she would receive what the caller described as "the lowdown on why Cedric Bartholomew had to die." When she arrived at The Lodge, she was met not by a woman but by a man who pointed a gun at her and said she was a nuisance that he intended to end right then.

And then into the room came a man of immense bravery. Detective Sergeant Rayyan Padgett, armed with nothing but his warrant card and his courage, stepped in front of the reporter and demanded her would-be killer hand over his gun.

It is with the greatest sadness that I have to tell you that the man holding the reporter hostage shot the brave detective. Then into the room burst Detective Constable Nicola Hayward, also unarmed. What happened next the reporter was unable to tell us because that was the moment she made her escape.

We will be in close touch with Batterton police station ready to report to readers the moment new information emerges.

It was a grim meeting of the Major Crime Investigation Team. Blazeley said, 'I could murder that bloody woman. One of our best officers is bleeding to death and it's *her* fault, and what does she do? She buggers off leaving Nicola with the other one.'

Theresa said, 'She must be the one writing this blog?'

'Of course she is,' said Susanna. 'But we've been in touch with Facebook and Twitter and they refuse to identify the owner of the accounts. And the company in Kazakhstan just hangs up the phone.'

Blazeley said, 'Enough about her. Who is at the hospital with Rayyan?'

'Nicola,' said Susanna. 'Who else? She holds herself responsible for not stopping him until armed backup was there.'

'She should be home in bed.'

'I'm not going to be the one to tell her that.'

'How does it look?'

'Not good.'

'Shit. All right, what's done is done. Sometimes you just have to hand things over to the Almighty and say, "Sort that out." Rayyan's parents are dead. His next of kin is a brother. The brother's been informed. Thank God that job didn't fall to us. Let's get some work done.'

The reference to the Almighty had not escaped Susanna's notice. 'I didn't know you were a believer, Boss.'

'We're all believers when things get beyond human help, Susanna. Cantrell is in custody. He'll certainly be charged with attempted murder and if Rayyan doesn't make it that will change to murder. Can we prove he shot Westwood, too?'

'Nicola was there. We've taken her statement. Got the clothes she was wearing, too.'

'Does Cantrell have a lawyer? He doesn't strike me as the kind to rely on a duty solicitor.'

'Strangely enough,' said Susanna, 'he's instructed the same lawyer as Jensen Bartholomew. And she's here, and giving a very good impression of patience as she waits for us to interview her client.'

'The kind of hourly rate she charges,' said Blazeley, 'I should think she's happy to wait. Gareth. Sally. Let's see what Cantrell has to say. I suspect he could unwrap this whole Bartholomew/Malinov/Ali Badaan thing if he felt like it. See if you can make him feel like it.' He turned to Susanna. 'Nicola isn't the only one who can tell us what happened. That damn reporter was there. Get her in here.'

* * *

The nurses had given Nicola a seat where she was unlikely to be disturbed. Rayyan was still in surgery; apart from that, they could tell her nothing. Then a man and a woman approached her. The man had the same eyes as Rayyan, and was roughly the same age. He said, 'You're here for Rayyan?'

She nodded. 'I'm his colleague.'

'And I'm his brother. I gather there's no news.'

'Nothing. I'm going to be honest – I saw him before he went in and it didn't look good.'

The woman said, 'Excuse me asking, but you're not Nicola by any chance?'

She nodded again. 'Nicola Hayward.'

'I thought so. Rayyan talked about you.'

'Oh?'

'He likes you,' said Rayyan's brother.

'A lot,' said his wife.

'We shouldn't be telling you that.'

'But we are,' said the woman, 'because we think it's a waste. And if Rayyan makes it through this, the waste needs to stop.'

'Lizzie!'

'Well, I'm sorry, Amran, but it needs to be said.' She took Nicola's hand in hers. 'Rayyan fancies the hell out of you. But he won't tell you so. That's how the Padgett men are.' She jerked her head in her husband's direction. 'This one was exactly the same. If I hadn't given him a damn good nudge, he'd still be mooning over me and keeping his trap shut.'

'What? Nudge? When?'

'See? He didn't even notice.'

Amran said, 'We only know Rayyan's side of the story, Lizzie. For all you know, Nicola is in love with someone else.'

'Of course she is. That's why she's sitting here with eyes red raw from weeping. Men!'

Nicola was thinking about the conversations she'd had with her sister, Sasha. How she'd fantasised about Rayyan as a partner. How she'd worried that she might make a move only to be repulsed. How she'd thought that Rayyan probably wouldn't want to be involved with someone from work, without giving him the chance to say so. Lizzie was right. If Rayyan got out of here alive, things were going to change.

Lizzie said, 'Shall I see I can find three coffees? It looks like we might be here for a while.'

* * *

Sally set up the recording equipment and everyone present identified themselves. To Susanna and Blazeley watching on a monitor, Cantrell's supercilious calmness was like an insult. This man had tried to kill one of their own and they might yet learn that he had succeeded. So many people felt they were above the law. Cantrell looked as though he was one of them.

Sally said, 'Mr Cantrell. I'd like to remind you of two things. The first is that you have been arrested on suspicion of involvement in the attempted murder of Detective Sergeant Rayyan Padgett. The latest information we have is that that charge may soon become a charge of murder. The second is that you are still under caution, which I'm now going to repeat.'

Susanna said, 'Did you see that? His eyes didn't flicker.'

'We are dealing with a psychopath,' said Blazeley. 'I wonder if they'll go for insanity as a defence.'

Sally said, 'Did you shoot Detective Sergeant Padgett?'

The lack of even a glance between Cantrell and his lawyer told the watchers that Helena Booth had briefed him well. He shook his head. 'No. Of course I didn't.'

'Did you shoot Thomas Westwood?'

Cantrell's eyebrows rose. 'Who is Thomas Westwood?'

Gareth said, 'Did you shoot anyone today?'

Cantrell shook his head. 'Not today or any other day.'

'Why where you at The Lodge?'

'I was invited.'

'By…?'

'Well, that's the interesting thing. I thought the invitation came from Jensen Bartholomew. But what happened at that place suggested otherwise. It's your job to ask questions and mine to answer them. I know that. But would you like to know what I think?'

Sally adopted a completely blank expression – something both interviewers had perfected over the years. 'Please, Mr Cantrell. What do you think?'

Cantrell leaned forward as though about to convey vital information. 'I think someone was trying to set me up.'

'And who might want to do that?'

'If I knew, I'd tell you.'

'This invitation purporting to be from Jensen Bartholomew. What did it say?'

'Simply that he had business matters to discuss.'

'Had you done business with Mr Bartholomew in the past?'

'No. At least, not to my knowledge. But I know him, of course. And so, when I got the invitation…'

'You know Mr Bartholomew. How did that come about?'

'Oh, sometimes we move in the same circles.'

'The same circles?'

'Government circles. Ministers, senior civil servants, influencers. Lobbyists. Bartholomew is acquainted with some of the people I'm acquainted with myself. I expect you know how these things work.'

Gareth said, 'You mentioned discussing business matters. What business are you in?'

Cantrell waved a hand. 'Oh. This and that. I suppose you'd call me a facilitator. I make things happen. For the benefit of this country and the people who live in it.'

'We have recovered the gun that we believe was used in the shooting of Detective Sergeant Padgett and Thomas Westwood. When you were arrested, your fingerprints and DNA were taken. It's early days, of course, and our scenes of crime officers will be hard at work for days yet. Possibly weeks. But what we have established so far is that the gun that was used to shoot both men has your fingerprints on it. And no others. Can you explain how that happened?'

Cantrell said, 'It must be my gun.'

Sally said, 'You have a gun?'

'Oh, yes. It's registered. I belong to a gun club. That's the only place I use it – I fire it at targets. I keep it there, too.'

'The gun is yours. It has only your fingerprints on it. It was used today to shoot two men. You say you weren't the person who fired the gun. Can you explain how it came to be used? If not you, who did fire it? Who had access to it?'

'Until today, I would have answered that question by saying that only I had access to it. But, clearly, that would be wrong. I haven't been to the gun club for two weeks and so I haven't needed to look at the gun.' He spread out his hands as if despairing of finding the answer. 'Equally clearly, someone stole it. The same someone, I think we can assume, who sent me the invitation purporting to be from Jensen Bartholomew.'

'I see,' said Sally. 'And why would someone want to do that?'

Cantrell's expression now suggested that Sally must be a little slow on the uptake. 'Why? So that they could kill someone and have me take the blame. Not your detective sergeant, of course – that is a terrible tragedy and I grieve for him almost as much as you must do. I can only pray that he recovers. No, not him – the other one.'

'Thomas Westwood?'

'If that is his name. As I said, I know nothing of him.'

Gareth's phone buzzed. He looked at the message and then said, 'What about Bernadette Spence? Do you know anything of her?'

They could only marvel at Cantrell's range of expressions. This time he exuded puzzlement. 'Bernadette? Spence? No, I don't think I… Who is she?'

Gareth said, 'Mr Cantrell, we're going to have you taken back to your cell. There are things we need to discuss with senior officers.'

Helena Booth spoke for the first time. 'Can you give me any idea of timescales here? Should I check into a local hotel?'

Sally said, 'Ms Booth, we must leave decisions like that to you. But I think you can take it that we will wish to speak to Mr Cantrell a number of times over the next day or so.'

Cantrell said, 'If you allow me to go to the gun club, I can verify that my gun has been stolen.'

'That's all right, sir,' said Sally. 'You've been arrested in connection with a very serious offence. That has a number of consequences, one of which is that scenes of crime officers will be examining your house, your office, and everywhere else connected with you for evidence. They're probably there right now.'

As they stood up, she and Gareth and the two more senior officers watching on monitors saw Cantrell's careless façade slip. Blazeley said to Susanna, 'His brief hasn't warned him about that. And he's worried. Get onto the Met and ask them to tell whoever is crime scene manager that there is definitely something to find.'

CHAPTER 25

Time in the hospital seemed to go agonisingly slowly. Conversation drifted away and the three waiting people seemed sunk in their own silent thoughts.

For Nicola, things were crystallising. If Rayann was returned to them, she would hug him and never let him go. She'd worried too much about the dangers of dating someone from work and about what her mother would say. It was her life, and she'd lead it her way. And if Rayann didn't want her? She'd cross that bridge when she came to it. But he'd have to refuse her – she was going to stop making that decision on his behalf.

She thought about moments when it could have gone another way. The time when they were investigating a string of murders and managed to find time late one evening for pizza and beer. She'd kissed him – but only on the cheek. She'd thought of taking it further and then backed away. And what about the times she'd made him blush? Rayyan blushed so easily – she wanted more than she wanted anything in the world to see him blush again.

289

At last, a doctor came to where they were. If time had been going slowly, now it had stopped. She knew what that expression on his face meant. And she couldn't bear it.

The doctor said, 'The next of kin?'

Amran stood. 'I'm his brother.'

The doctor nodded. No doubt he had done this many times before, but still the pain was obvious. He said, 'I'm very sorry. We tried very hard. The damage was too great.'

Amran said, 'He's definitely gone?'

'I'm afraid so. I'm… Look. All we can ever say in these circumstances is that we are sorry. And of course we are. But I know how useless that must feel to you now. It will take a few minutes to clean him up, and then you can see him. In the meantime, if you'd like it, a chaplain is available.'

But Nicola was never going to see Rayann again. And she certainly wasn't going to talk to a chaplain. She was walking to the door, and along the corridor, and down the stairs, and out of the hospital.

If you'd asked her later to tell you what happened in those few minutes, she couldn't have answered. She sent a text message to Susanna to say that Rayann was dead and that she needed a while before she came to the station.

Then she rang her sister. 'I'm at the hospital, Sasha. I don't trust myself to drive. Can you please come and get me?'

Sasha had read the story in The Post. She didn't need to

ask what had happened. 'Stay right where you are. I'll be there in ten.'

* * *

When Gareth and Sally reached the room in which interviews were monitored, Sally said, 'He's asked for time with his brief.'

'I bet he has,' said Blazeley. 'He's rattled. He wasn't banking on SOCO turning his home over. He's going to have something to tell us because he's going to want to make a deal. Get back there quickly and let the solicitor know that we will be rearresting his client, this time on suspicion of involvement in the murder of a police officer.'

'Oh, no,' said Gareth. 'Poor Rayyan.'

'Poor Nicola,' said Sally. 'Now she'll see what's been obvious to everyone else.'

'And when you've done that,' said Blazeley, 'take a statement from Bernadette Spence. And impress on her that she is not writing a story for the paper. We want the facts and we only want the facts. But we want them all. And make sure she knows that if she writes another word about what happened in that building before Cantrell and anyone else involved has been tried and found guilty, she'll be in court herself for perverting the course of justice.'

At that point, a uniformed sergeant appeared in the room. 'A farmer has found a body in the gateway to one of his fields. It's a woman and her throat was shot. I'm telling you because the gateway is on the road to The Lodge, it isn't very far away, and the body has been identified as Mary Spilling, housekeeper at Jamaica House.'

'Well,' said Blazeley. 'All the bits of the jigsaw are coming together. SOCO are on the scene?'

'Yes, they are.'

'Thanks, Bill. Good work.'

* * *

Helena Booth didn't want to make this phone call from her hotel room or from her personal phone. It took her some time to find a public phone box away from any of the places she had frequented on this trip. She put a call through to the senior partner at her law firm. When they had both hung up, the partner rang an old friend he always addressed as EG. It stood for *eminence grise* and all most people knew about EG was that he had a seat in the House of Lords and was frequently consulted by the Prime Minister. They knew each other well; they'd been at school together, something they shared with Cantrell, and they belonged to the same club, which is where they now agreed to meet.

EG said, 'Cantrell. I suppose he is guilty.'

'Guilty of what? In Helena's view, there's no doubt he shot two men today. One of them was no loss to anyone, but the other was a police officer and you know what kind of publicity killing a policeman brings with it. But if that was all he was guilty of, I'd say, let him go down for it. London won't be a poorer place if Cantrell disappears from sight for twenty years. Quite the opposite, some would say. And when he gets out he can do the usual thing… announce he's found God; set up soup kitchens or something; do the TV rounds talking about how prison saved him from himself. '

'So what are you worrying about?'

'*I* am not worrying about anything. I'm simply doing my patriotic duty by pointing out things that you ought to be worried about.'

'Me?'

'People who depend on you. Scenes of crime officers are turning over Cantrell's flat in Mayfair. There's no point trying to block it, because that will only pull down public attention. The days when your friends in high places could do stuff like that and get away with it are gone. According to Cantrell, they'll find evidence that ties Jensen Bartholomew not only to conspiracy to murder his brother, but also to trade in banned goods. *American* banned goods.'

'The PM won't like that.'

293

'He will if he can draw its teeth. If he can show that he is taking action before Washington knows anything about it.'

'What sort of action?'

'Jenny Frobisher is in this up to her ears.'

'Ah.'

'Not only has she taken money from Bartholomew without declaring it, she's also been in the pay of some extremely unpleasant people in Teheran.'

'Good grief. And the police are going to find evidence of this?'

'The evidence is certainly there.'

'Right. I know what to do. What does Cantrell want in exchange?'

'Cantrell has always known that a day like this may come.'

'He has a bolt hole prepared?'

'A place to run to. A whole new identity. Enough money to live there in the style to which he is accustomed for at least two lifetimes.'

'Won't the police find out all about that?'

'It isn't in his flat. It's in a bank in Grand Cayman.'

'So he wants…?'

'To be moved from Batterton. Ostensibly to a place where he can be held more securely. But in a car – not a secure police van.'

'And we are supposed to let that move be interrupted? You don't think that will look a bit suspicious?'

'I think you need to consider the alternative. And Cantrell can recommend a private firm that can do the interrupting.'

'You're not suggesting that we contract with them?'

'Of course not.'

'Well, thank you, Geoffrey. I shall talk to the appropriate people and someone with more to lose than me or you will make the decision.'

* * *

When he got the first batch of evidence from the SOCOs examining Cantrell's Mayfair flat, Blazeley phoned Helena Booth to say that he was re-arresting Jensen Bartholomew. She said, 'Can you do that?'

'This is on a different matter.'

'Which is…?'

'I only have faxed copies at the moment. The originals are on their way to us. But they were found in Mr Cantrell's flat and they make it clear that Jensen Bartholomew lied to us when he said he had had no part in trading embargoed goods with Iran. We knew the documents existed – they were removed from the files stolen from Patel and

Mayfield. Which makes it likely, by the way, that after being stolen those files have been in Mr Cantrell's possession. We're going to want to talk to him about that. But he's already in custody, so that can wait until we have the originals and we've been able to examine them for fingerprints. In the meantime, we want Bartholomew's response to these new allegations.'

'Is he with you now?'

'I expect him within the next ten minutes.'

'I'll be there as soon as I can. You won't start interviewing him until I've been able to talk to him.' It wasn't a question.

While he waited for Gareth and Sally to be able to interview Jensen Bartholomew, Blazeley discussed with Susanna information coming in from SOCO. 'Westwood had a gun in his possession when he died. There are two sets of prints on the gun. One set belongs to Dominic Carter, but he's dead and his bum's cold so we can be sure he didn't kill her. The other set belongs to Westwood.'

'Westwood took it from Carter when he killed him.'

'That seems most likely. Westwood also had a knife, with blood on it. We'll have confirmation as soon as the lab gets through with it, but it seems to me there's a very high chance that the blood belongs to Mary Spilling. Then there's the key. SOCO have identified it as the key to Cedric

Bartholomew's house. They found Jensen Bartholomew's prints on it.'

'But it was in Westwood's pocket? That's it! We've got Bartholomew. Westwood let himself into Cedric Bartholomew's house with a key. We never asked where he got it from. Jensen Bartholomew must have given it to him.'

The phone on Blazeley's desk rang. He picked it up, listened and said, 'Sure. I'll talk to her. But she can't come here – I'll come down. Set aside an interview room for us.' To Susanna he said, 'Let's go.'

'Go where?'

Helena Booth wants to talk to us. She's not a stupid woman and she can see the strength of the evidence against her clients. As I said earlier, Cantrell is going to want to make a deal.'

But that was not, in fact, the subject Helena Booth wanted to discuss. She said, 'I can no longer represent Jensen Bartholomew.'

'Ms Booth, if he's admitted guilt to you, you need to tell us that.'

'He's admitted nothing. It's a question of conflict of interest.'

Blazeley had that wonderful sense only occasionally experienced that the dam was about to break. 'Say some more.'

'Mr Cantrell is prepared to provide you with evidence implicating Jensen Bartholomew in the murder of his brother, Cedric. I cannot represent two clients who are testifying against each other. Obviously. I have to choose, I've spoken to my senior partner, and we have decided that Mr Bartholomew will have to find another legal representative.'

'Yes. I see. And Mr Cantrell will provide this evidence against Mr Bartholomew… When?'

'Tomorrow morning. I shall be staying in Batterton overnight and I would be grateful if an interview with Mr Cantrell could be arranged for ten in the morning. I shall be here thirty minutes before that, and I would like to spend those thirty minutes consulting with my client.'

'His custody clock is ticking. We can make those arrangements, but we wouldn't be able to drag things out any further without charging him. And Jensen Bartholomew?'

'I can do nothing further for Mr Bartholomew.'

* * *

Watching Jensen Bartholomew as the custody sergeant told him that Helena Booth was no longer able to represent him, and then told him why, was like seeing the air leave a balloon. The custody sergeant reported to Blazeley, 'He looked ten years older.'

'What does he want to do about a lawyer?'

'He's going to use the duty solicitor. It's Cyril Bonser today.'

Susanna said, 'That's a bit of a comedown after Helena Booth.'

'He's giving up,' said Blazeley. 'He knows, if Cantrell is giving evidence against him, it's all over. But with any luck he'll want revenge.'

'Cantrell gives us Bartholomew and in return Bartholomew gives us Cantrell?'

'We can only hope. Let's get Gareth and Sally in there as soon as Bonser turns up. And let Maisie in Forensic Accounting have sight of these documents.'

CHAPTER 26

Sally put three photocopied documents on the table. She said, 'I am showing Mr Bartholomew exhibit CD/1. Mr Bartholomew, what do you see here?'

Bartholomew sank even lower in his chair. He looked at Cyril Bonser sitting beside him. Bonser said, 'I'd like a moment with my client. And then he would like to make a statement, which I will prepare for him.'

'Of course,' said Sally. 'But before you do that, and so that you can be sure that your client is telling us everything he needs to tell us, I'd like to show him exhibit TW/1.' And she placed an evidence bag onto the table. 'Mr Bartholomew. This is a key to Cedric Bartholomew's front door. It was found in the pocket of Thomas Westwood. We have reason to believe that Thomas Westwood killed Cedric Bartholomew and that, in order to do so, he opened Cedric Bartholomew's door with this key. The key, as we might expect, has Thomas Westwood's fingerprints on it. It was in your pocket. When you are preparing your statement with Mr Bonser's assistance, will you please include an explanation of how that came to be? Unless you can persuade us otherwise, we will be informing the Crown Prosecution Service that we believe you gave the key to Thomas Westwood when you instructed him to kill your brother.'

* * *

Next morning, when Helena Booth arrived at the police station to speak to Cantrell, Susanna was able to tell her that Jensen Bartholomew had been charged, among other offences, with conspiracy to murder his brother, Cedric Bartholomew. 'We have his full confession. I'm sure the duty solicitor who took your place told him the gig was up. I've no doubt he hopes that pleading guilty will reduce his tariff. He states in his confession that your client joined him in that conspiracy and that it was your client who found Thomas Westwood and instructed him to carry out the murder.

'Thank you for telling me that, Inspector. I have no doubt that my client will dispute that allegation.'

And so it proved. When Cantrell and Helena came into the interview room, Helena said, 'I shall read a statement on behalf of my client. That will be my client's complete account of the matter and he will answer no questions.' The statement contained explanations for every circumstance the police found questionable, and denied Jensen Bartholomew's accusation of complicity in Cedric Bartholomew's murder. Sally and Gareth went upstairs to be instructed by Blazeley and Susanna, and returned to tell Cantrell that the Crown Prosecution Service had authorised them to charge him with murder and conspiracy to murder, that he would be taken in front of a magistrate, and that he would then be remanded in custody. Then the officers most central to the investigation met while their colleagues left to carry on with other investigations into other serious crimes.

Rayann's death still overshadowed everything. It was the first time since Rayyan's death that Nicola had been into the police station. She was white faced but waved away suggestions that she take a few days holiday. 'I'd just sit and mope. I'm better off here. Do you think we've got them both?'

Susanna said, 'Bartholomew will certainly go down. We've got his confession. His brother's killing was premeditated and carefully planned and he had a central part in it. There won't be any question of settling for a manslaughter charge – he's looking at a life sentence. But Cantrell? I'm not so sure. What do you think, Boss?'

Blazeley shook his head. 'Nicola and Bernadette Spence are eyewitnesses to both murders. Cantrell hasn't a hope of acquittal, even though whatever barrister they choose for the defence is going to be the pick of the bunch.

Theresa said, 'What about Annabelle Tomkins? Also known as Becky Smith?'

Susanna said, 'What did she do that we could charge her with? Give a false name and untrue information to a journalist? How many people in this country do that every single day of the week? And how many journalists do it back to them?'

'She was on the wrong side.'

'Yes,' said Blakiston, 'she was. And there are many countries where being on the wrong side can get you thrown in jail. Or worse. And in those countries it's the state that decides which is the wrong side and which the right. Fortunately, that isn't how we work here. If we put our minds to it, I'm sure we could charge her with obstructing the police and wasting police time. But if we did that, we'd be wasting police time ourselves. She's a very unpleasant person with a monumental sense of entitlement but in this country we don't send people to jail for that.'

Susanna said, 'We've also got Del Theobald, of course. He admitted hitting Yuri Malinov on the head and Malinov died of it.'

Blakiston said, 'If he gets a good enough barrister, he might get away with manslaughter instead of murder. Even so, we've taken him off the streets for a few years.'

'Uniform will be grateful for that,' said Theresa. 'Can we do anything about this blog Bernadette Spence is running?'

'We can once we can prove it's hers. The evidence right now is very clear but it's also circumstantial and the CPS doesn't like cases based only on circumstantial evidence.'

There was a short spell of lighter humour when someone brought in that evening's late edition of *The Post*.

MP Loses the Whip

Bernadette Spence

The whole of Batterton was shocked this evening when Downing Street announced that the whip had been withdrawn from Batterton's MP, Jenny Frobisher. No reason was announced, but a separate press release said that the Home Office has passed documents to Scotland Yard. Mrs Frobisher told this reporter that any suggestion she had been involved in illegal activity was entirely without foundation and that she was the victim of a witch hunt. She said she has been proud to represent Batterton at Westminster for the past eight years and that she would continue to do so as an independent.

'So that's what that's about,' said Blazeley. 'The Super told me he'd been called in by the Chief Constable and told something would be blowing up and that we were to leave it alone. The Met are going to be handling it.'

'That should ensure an almighty cock-up,' said Susanna. 'I suppose they'll want to move him down there.'

'The Met will take care of that. We don't need to be involved.'

* * *

When they left the station that evening, Theresa and Susanna each invited Nicola to come home with them. She shook her head. 'I'm staying the next couple of nights at my sister's place.' But she did agree to a drink in a nearby pub before going home. Blazeley, Gareth and Sally joined them.

Jamie had been home more than an hour when Theresa got there and he had a shepherd's pie in the oven. He'd always been a better cook than Theresa and she was more than happy to let him get on with it. He left the kitchen as she came through the front door and hugged her. 'It's all over. I heard. Well done.'

She said, 'It was strange. There was no feeling of celebration because Rayann's death overshadows everything. I suppose it'll be like that for a while yet.'

Although neither of them knew it, Detective Superintendent Chris McAvoy also did the cooking in the house he shared with DI Susanna David. Dinner there tonight was a smoked haddock risotto. He handed her a glass of wine, wrapped his arms around her and said, 'I expect you'd like to shower before we eat. But the Chief Constable will be on TV in two minutes, so let's sit and listen to that first.'

It was almost the end of local television's regular evening show. They'd just covered the story of puppies being trained to be guide dogs and the regular anchor was smiling and wrinkle-eyed as he looked at the camera. Then, in one of those total changes that only television anchors seem able truly to master, his face became a picture of sadness and solemnity. 'Policeman Rayyan Padgett was shot dead yesterday. We invited the chief constable to comment, and she asked for the opportunity to speak to us all. At this sad time, we were only too happy to agree. Chief Constable.'

Susanna had a lump in her throat as she watched the chief constable pause before speaking. Looking straight into the camera without appearing to need any notes she said, 'Rayyan Padgett was a detective sergeant in Batterton and a valued part of the Major Crime Investigation Team. He died when he came to the aid of a member of the public who was being threatened by an armed gunman. The member of the public survived, thanks to Rayyan, and the gunman is under arrest. Everyone in Batterton can, as a result, feel safer tonight. The price of that safety was Rayyan's life.

'I've been asked several times today why Rayyan, who was completely unarmed, would take on an armed man. Is it not true, people have asked, that our police officers are told not to challenge armed suspects? That they are instructed to wait for the arrival of armed backup? The only answer I can give is that we don't as yet know what happened. There will be an investigation and I wouldn't want anything I say now to prejudice that. But sometimes, for any police officer, there will come a time when a higher rule must govern their actions. We have heard many stories in recent years of police malfeasance. Of officers doing things they should not do, sometimes at great harm to the public. What we hear much less often is that, for every officer caught doing something wrong, there are several hundred who go out every day and do exactly what they are employed to do. They protect the public, sometimes at great risk to themselves. Sometimes, indeed, they don't go home that night. Or any night thereafter. We don't hear much about these people, because someone doing her or his job and doing it well isn't news. Well, let us all this evening hold Detective Sergeant Rayyan Padgett in our minds.

'More than a hundred years ago, A E Housman wrote an epitaph for the British soldiers who died at Ypres. These were not conscripts. They were not men called up from other occupations. They were the British Expeditionary Force – regulars, professional soldiers who had pledged to give their lives if necessary in defence of their country. At Ypres and in battles that followed, every one of them paid the ultimate price. Just as Rayyan Padgett did. I'd like to read Housman's words to you.' And then, without once looking anywhere but at the screen, she said,

'These, in the days when heaven was falling,

The hour when earth's foundations fled,

Followed their mercenary calling

And took their wages and are dead.

Their shoulders held the sky suspended;

They stood, and earth's foundations stay;

What God abandoned, these defended,

And saved the sum of things for pay.

'They saved the sum of things for pay. And the people of this country have them to thank for the lives they have lived in freedom. Rayyan Padgett did the same. And the people of Batterton, as they go about their lives in peace, may wish to remember him. Thank you.'

Susanna knew that there were tears in her eyes. She looked at Chris and saw them in his, too. There was nothing more to say. 'I'll take that shower now.'

POSTSCRIPT

A few days later, at a time when the eyes of the whole country were focused on reports that a member of the royal family had been stripped of his titles and duties, a press release was slipped out saying that Cantrell had overpowered the driver of the vehicle carrying him to London and that his whereabouts were at present unknown. The public were warned that he was likely to be dangerous and should not be approached. Questions about why he had not been transported in a secure prison van from which only an audacious attack could have sprung him were left unanswered.

In Batterton, Nicola Hayward was appointed Detective Sergeant in the Major Crimes Squad and a new detective constable joined from Wolverhampton. Nicola and Theresa were between them instructed to help him get acquainted with Batterton as quickly as possible.

Three months later, Bernadette Spence decided it was time for a follow-up on the Cantrell story, but she found the Home Office and the Prison Service unhelpful. The escaped prisoner was still at large. Yes, of course they were looking for him, and an announcement would be made as soon as he was recaptured. No, they didn't think there was anything suspicious about his escape; it was just one of those things that happen in a world that isn't always as orderly as we might like.

And Theresa had news for Jamie. His face wreathed in smiles, he said, 'Are you sure?'

'No, Jamie. I'm not sure. What I am sure of is that I've been as regular as clockwork since I was a girl and now I'm running late. It might mean nothing, so we're not going to tell anyone yet, are we? But you might want to brace yourself for the possibility that you may be going to be a father.'

'I can't wait!'

'Well, my darling, I'm afraid you'll have to. That's how it works in these matters.'

FROM THE AUTHOR

I hope you enjoyed this. If you did, you may like to know that *Drawn to Murder*, the first book in the *Batterton Police Series*, is already available and the third in the series, *Murder Under Surveillance*, will be published on 1 July, 2022. Here are some other books I've written that you may like:

Books Written as John Lynch

Sharon Wright: Butterfly
No one gives Sharon a chance – except Sharon

A crime novel set in gritty South London and rural France. Sharon woos the way a female mantis might – knowing that, when she's done, the male may have to die.

Darkness Comes
Ted Bailey stares Death in the face. And Death blinks first

Ted Bailey has got away with drug dealing, gunrunning, and even murder. Now he faces the ultimate judge. A death sentence, surely? But all is not as it seems.

The Making of Billy McErlane

Born into the family from hell. Destined for a life of crime. In prison at 14. But Billy's life is not over yet.

A coming-of-age story that begins in tragedy and ends in hope. A bittersweet story of love, loss and one young man's refusal to accept what life offers.

Books written as R J Lynch

The James Blakiston Series

A Just and Upright Man and Poor Law
(with more to come)

Set in the north-east of England in the 1760s, the James Blakiston Series is historical fiction from the point of view of people at the bottom of the social heap and not the top.

Printed in Great Britain
by Amazon